ELDERBERRY
FLUTE SONG

ELDERBERRY FLUTE SONG

CONTEMPORARY COYOTE TALES

By Peter Blue Cloud
Illustrated by Bill Crosby

THE CROSSING PRESS / Trumansburg, New York 14886

ACKNOWLEDGMENTS

A special thanks to Gary Lawless of Blackberry Press who published two chapbooks of
mine in which much of this material first appeared: *Coyote And Friends,* 1976, and *Back
Then Tomorrow,* 1978.

I also wish to mention and thank such pub-
lications as "Co-Evolution Quarterly," "Contact II," "Greenfield Review," "Kuksu," and
the anthology *The Remembered Earth.*

Good wishes to Bill Crosby, whose first
drawings of coyote and fox sent my imagination whirling.

May Coyote continue to support the small
presses which are really the big ones.

Peter Blue Cloud

Library of Congress Cataloging in Publication Data

Blue Cloud, Peter.
    Elderberry flute song.

    1. Trickster. 2. Indians of North America--Legends.
I. Title.
E98.F6B58   398.2'452974442'0897   82-4965
ISBN 0-89594-070-1   AACR2
ISBN 0-89594-069-8 (pbk.)

Contents

ELDERBERRY FLUTE SONG

The Cry

It was all darkness and always had been.
There was nothing there forever.
Creation was a tiny seed
awaiting a dream.
    The dream came to be
because of the cry.
A howling cry which was
an echo in the emptiness of nothing.
The cry was very lonely and
caused the dream to
turn over in its sleep.
The dream did not want to awaken,
but the crying would not stop.
    Well, thought the dream, opening its mind,
so now I am awake and there is something.
The dream floated above itself
and looked into its mind.
It wanted to see what the cry was.
    What it saw was a dream
within its own dreaming.
And that other dream was Creation.
And Creation was the cry
seeking to begin something,
but it didn't know what,
and that is why it cried.
    So the original dream lifted
the Creation dream from its mind
and set it free.
Then it went to the other end of nothing
and let itself go back
to dreamless sleep.
    Creation floated all over the nothing,
dreaming of all the things it would do.
Its dreaming was interrupted
often by crying.

So, it wasn't me crying after all,
Creation thought.
Then it thought again,
but it is me because I dreamed it.
So, I have begun Creation with a cry.
    When I begin to create the universe,
I must remember to give the cry
a very special place.
    Perhaps
I'll call the cry
                Coyote.

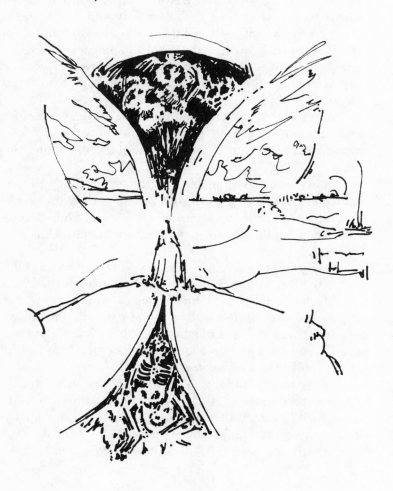

I Cry Often and Long

"There is a great aloneness in me, swirling like captured smoke within. I look around and look around again. It is an emptiness now, this land. It is an emptiness of the dead creatures and plants. It is a ghost land, a spirit land of keening winds. And the winds are the voices, the whispering sorrow of creations gone before their time.

"I cry often and long, but none of my relatives hear or answer. I am a grey shadow passing swiftly between naked stone. I reflect myself on the underbelly of a cloud. I am what you think you saw behind a blackened stump. I disperse myself in morning mist. I am the cry you hear in the black and soundless night. I am the dry and snapping twig of your uneasy sleep. I am the one who watches you from many eyes and directions.

"I cry often and long, and the feast I bring you is often an empty basket, rotted and useless. I am you when you fear to gaze at your reflection. I am a pair of cracked and bleeding feet.

"I cry often and long, and my cry is the echo of the anguished cry you hide in your own breast. I walk the many footpaths of your fears. I am the offspring of your childless marriage. I am the parent you feared and hated. I am your deathsong.

"I cry often and long, because you were never a child. I mourn the fact of your empty seed. I am part of the mystery you refuse to recognize. I am waiting for you. I am waiting for you and have been waiting for you from the time of your great-great-grandfather's parched lips. I am waiting for the promise you once gave to a land and a people. I am waiting for the return feast I gave your unborn children.

"I cry often and long. I have prophesied you running on all fours and partaking of grasses and herbs. I have visioned you mating in frenzy the wind and stars. I have dreamed your descent into naked-limbed beginnings. I have been devouring the flesh of your customs. I have gnawed your bones and sucked the marrow of your countless fears. I taste the bitterness of bile.

"I cry often and long. This robe I spread before this campfire is for your warmth. Why do you stand way back there in the shadows and cold?

"Come here; yes, that's it, slowly. Yes, now take my hand. Yes, now sit, stop trembling. Gently now, this robe I place about you, softly. There.

"It is done,
now sleep, and do not fear your dreaming."
❧

The Burden Basket

When asked, "Just what is night, anyway?"
Coyote closed his eyes,
placed his burden basket over his head
and began making the sounds of hoot owl.
"So, that is night!"
his nephew ventured,
eyeing his uncle doubtfully.
"No, nephew," Coyote said,
removing the burden basket from his head,
"that is someone trying to show night
in a foolish way."
"Well, then," nephew began, but
Coyote quickly picked up a big stick
and hit his nephew over the head.
Nephew fell and sat on the ground stunned.
After recovering somewhat,
he reached for the burden basket
and drew it over himself.
Nephew's younger brother
had watched all this in silence.
Coyote had long since gone his way.
It was growing dark,
the sky was an emptiness,
a blackness filled all space to bursting.
Younger brother thought to lift the basket
to see if his brother was all right.
The stars of the Sky Path spilled out.
He dropped the basket,
but curiosity won out,
and again he lifted it,
and the moon was within,
eclipsed by the basket's rim.
He raised the basket further
and the moon tumbled out
and went rolling into space.

He looked inside the basket and saw
that darkest night now lived
in the basket.

His brother wasn't within.
    So this is why
they make burden baskets,
he thought, sitting down
and drawing the basket
    over his head.

When the Sun Was Very Young

it lived inside of a big mountain. It had a breathing hole which opened on a plain where the rabbit people lived.

Coyote used to hunt the rabbits on that plain. He used to piss down their burrows to drive them out. No one could stand his rank piss for very long.

One day while he was hunting, he spotted the breathing hole of the sun and so he pissed down there. When nothing emerged, he put his ear close to the hole to listen. He heard a far-off rumbling. It must be a very big rabbit, he thought.

So he went and drank half a river and peed that down the hole. Steam started coming out of the hole. Then the ground rumbled and shook.

Coyote ran away. That was no rabbit, he decided; that must be some kind of monster. He hid behind a sagebrush to watch.

The mountain split open and the sun shot up into the sky. There was daylight!

Coyote looked at his penis, then patted it affectionately, "Oh, you are very powerful," he said. "Only you can make things like that happen."

And that's how things used to be in the old days.

❖

Why the Moon Dies

"I'm going to change the night. I don't like it with the moon always there in one place. It's too bright. We need darkness to hunt. We need it to sleep, too. Yes, I'm going to make some changes." Coyote Old Man said.

Coyote Old Woman was stirring-up a salmon soup. She looked at the old man and told him, "You'd better not fool around with the moon. You know that she's a woman and my sister, and that you should leave her alone. She's there for a purpose, you know."

"Well, I guess I should know, after all it was me who put her up there. At least I think it was me.

"I'm going to send my cousin Wolf up there to eat her. Or at least chase her to the other side of darkness. I'm going to have my way. I usually do, you know."

Coyote Old Woman got mad then, "You always have to spoil things, don't you? If Wolf bites my sister I'm going to cut myself where you like it so much. I'm going to bleed and call her back. Don't forget, I have power, too!"

Wolf didn't want to go after Moon. But Coyote Old Man had too much power. Wolf moaned a sad song to Moon.

Then Wolf began chasing Moon to the other side of darkness, taking small bites out of her. He cried all the while. His tears fell to earth as the first snow.

Coyote Old Woman did as promised and cut herself. And when she did so, Moon reappeared from the opposite side of darkness, and Wolf was running backwards, spitting back the pieces of Moon until she became one again.

Coyote Old Man liked this fading out and rebirth of Moon, and so he directed Wolf to forever repeat his chase.

And all women since then bleed to bring back Moon.

And this is also why Wolf cries.

❖

Why Coyote Eats Gophers

Of course this happened long before the two-legged ones were created. And all the creatures used to talk together and get along pretty good. They even used to cook their food with fire, but as you know, fire-making had to be forgotten for a while when it was found that the two-leggeds were kind of crazy.

So, anyway, there was this terrible accident which took place because Coyote was practicing what he liked to call: fart-a-landslide. Yes, even back in those days Coyote was always doing strange or silly things which no one else would. And one of these things was to fill up on green onions, then drink a lot of water to work up a good stomach gas. Then Coyote would run to the mountains where there were a lot of loose rocks on various slopes, back up to a mountain, and let loose a big fart. Then he'd sit and watch the falling rocks.

Well, this one time he really let go and started an avalanche. And unfortunately, Gopher Old Man was down in the gully picking watercress when it happened, and he got buried. Coyote felt real bad and asked his Louse, "What shall I do? I killed my good friend, Gopher Old Man."

"Yes," said Louse, "you are always getting into trouble, aren't you? Well, you better go tell Gopher Woman what happened. She's a good woman . . . good-looking, too. Hmm. Yes, and she's a fine cook and has a nice comfortable house. Gonna be awful lonesome, that poor woman. Gonna be wanting a new husband pretty soon, I guess . . . Hey, Coyote, why don't you marry her? But first you better tell her what really happened. And don't tell her any lies, either!"

"Lie? Me? How can you even think such a thing? Don't I feed you and keep you warm? Don't I take you all over the place on my back? Louse, I think you are ungrateful."

So Coyote ran all the way to Gopher Woman's house to tell her the news, after she'd fed him, of course, and let him take a little nap.

"Yes," Coyote told her, "I met Gopher Old Man on the trail this morning. He was heading upriver and told me he was leaving you for good because you weren't nice enough to him. Said he was gonna marry a good-looking upriver girl and just stay up that way for good."

She was pretty upset, that woman, and cried a lot and needed someone to comfort her. Coyote hung around her place, playing his elderberry flute and singing sweet songs. He played with her eight or ten children, too, and, yes, she fell for him, and pretty soon they were spending the nights together close to the fire, beneath the same robe.

Then one night as they were going at it the way they do, what with rolling around and such, they accidently pushed one of the children in the fire. And before the child could even cry out, it was roasted nice and sweet smelling. And Coyote sat up a little later to light his pipe like he did, to sit quietly smoking after having made love.

Yes, he smelled that roasted gopher child and, "Hmmm, what's that good smell? Why, I do believe that good woman went and fixed something extra special. I better have a taste and find out if it's good." He took a taste. "Yum, yum, I do believe that I've never tasted anything so good before. Well, well, look here! It has bones!"

He sat thinking about it, licking the sweet juices from his fingers. He thought and thought; then he eyed the children

and went over and counted them. And sure enough, one was missing.

Next morning he ran outside, then came limping in when he knew that Gopher Woman was up. He was limping and groaning, as he told her how her child had gotten up in the night and told Coyote that he was leaving home to go look for his father. "And when I tried to stop him he dropped a big stone on my foot to keep me from following him." He rubbed his foot and groaned some more, while eyeing the children to see which was plumpest.

Then each night for three more nights, a child disappeared: "Going to find the old man," as Coyote put it.

But Gopher Woman was pretty smart, and she got kind of suspicious of Coyote. So one night she pretended to sleep and saw what Coyote was about to do. So she made him love her some more, and then more after that, so that Coyote got all tired and fell asleep.

And while he slept, Gopher Woman cut his penis off and dressed it in a child's clothing and threw it into the fire.

And Coyote, always hungry like he is, woke up soon after and had his usual snack; only it tasted different this time. And when he'd finished it, Gopher Woman jumped up and told him what he'd just eaten. Then she chased him from her house, hitting him with his own walking stick, and swearing never again to trust Coyote.

And Coyote, he still likes gopher meat, and he can't forget what a good lover Gopher Woman was. That's why he cries—they say he's still trying to win her back.

And of course Coyote got himself a new penis. But that was in another story.

❖

How Coyote Got His Penis Back

after that one time someone had taken it
away from him in anger.
                         "Well, this is
no fun at all." He told Coyote Woman,
and she agreed that she, too, kind of
missed it.
        So Coyote pulled Louse from himself
by the scruff of his neck and
demanded, "Well, where is it?"
        And Louse, who had just been
entertaining relatives in the forest
of Coyote's hair, got angry and
said, "Go chase a porcupine!" for
want of anything better to say.
(And, we *do* apologize to porcupine.)

So Coyote went looking for
Porcupine, and sure enough, there
went Porcupine, waddling along,
supporting himself with Coyote's
penis for a walking stick.
                    "Hey,
give that thing back to me!" Coyote
demanded from a respectful distance.
    Porcupine liked his new walking stick
and wouldn't give it up unless
they gambled for it.
    Well, they gambled for many days,
and all the while Porcupine leaned on
that penis, getting it all crooked
and bruised on the end.
    And by the time Coyote won
it back, it stayed crooked,
and sore when he put it on.
    It's still crooked, and always
itchy on the end, and that's why
Coyote's always wanting to
rub it
        somewhere.
❖

Sweat Song

Coyote
    running
running
    coyote

deserts
    of ice
rivers
    crystal pain
mountains
    breathing
        coyote

sweat bath
    cedar shadow
mirrow hawk
    dream feel
coyote coyote
    obsidian claws
hey, coyote
    hey, coyote

round house
    of coyote
mountains
    breathing
mirror hawk
    hey, coyote
cedar shadow
    hey, coyote

coyote
    running
running
    coyote

song
    done.

First Fire and the Myth of Sense

"At world's beginning it is said that Grandfather Coyote stole first fire, carrying the spark of living ember in a hollow section of antler filled with punk. Warmth was given us then and eyes of light in the darkness of that first cave, it is said. We are also told that first dreamer came to be because he was given to see into the fire and beyond. Do you deny this, Coyote, or is it indeed how things came to be as they are?"

"I deny nothing and all. It is said, and we are told, you tell me. Will you scratch these sayings on a piece of stone to be kept forever as a guide for the mind's feet when it is too busy to watch where it might be going? Better scratch an extra set of stones to be kept in a secluded cave for the benefit of other mighty thinkers and questioners such as yourself.

"It was many, many seasons after another world's beginning that first fire stole us, scorched us, I should say. It was the other creatures before us who took first fire and decided to light the whole of Creation. They wished to see the allness of Creation at one time, in one great, fiery setting. And set they did, the whole world of their puny habitation, on fire. And saw instead the stars and surrounding universe dim and fade in the brilliance of their doing. And burned and boiled the thinking matter encased within their thick skulls. And felt the bones and sinews of their proud bodies burned, blackened and brittled to crumbling. And their final vision was exactly as they'd wished and deserved; for pain and agony are the brightest fires of light and enlightenment known to any creature ever created.

"Grandfather carried a spark of light, all right! A burning coal of intense pain stuck fast between his toes. He ran to his cave to escape the pain, but like most pain given us for later meditation, it followed him in his flight. And call it what you will, pure chance or fortuitous occurrence, but the living coal was dislodged in that cave and smoldered on his grass bedding and caught and held and devoured the pile of sticks which were the ribs of his first (though he didn't know it at the time) sweat lodge. Okay, okay, enough, Grandfather said, in fact shouted, still trying to ease the almost unbearable pain, then sent his grandson out of the cave to gather more sticks to keep alive the cause of his pain in order for him to better study the blister forming between his toes.

"And it was, 'hey, this fire is nice and warm,' as grandson put it, and Grandfather grew angrier still, having decided to name fire OUCH! but stuck with *fire* because it was said aloud. And, 'well, well,' said Coyote Old Woman, 'I can see to grind acorn for the morning's mush, and so can sleep a little later mornings.' And Grandfather rubbed fish oil on his burn (and

thought, almost proudly, well, it is my burn) and heard his family's comments and sighed sadly, knowing that he'd once again been trapped into something he didn't really want to happen but would happen anyway, regardless of how he felt.

"And the pain having eased somewhat, Grandfather looked around the warm and lighted cave, sighing, aware of the consequences of this accidental and-so-forth. But he didn't say anything just then (and it wouldn't have done any good, anyway, if we but look at the way things tend to evolve) but merely walked himself in a circle several times and curled into a ball of sleep, still wary, but very weary, and just close enough to the fire to absorb some warmth without the danger of re-catching fire.

"Yes, the old fellow knew how the senses of smell and sight and the ability to live within the seasons, and even the sense of thinking, how all these would be lulled and lost in part or even wholly in the comfort brought by fire. And maybe he tossed and turned or snorted in apprehension while sleeping. He should have but didn't remember next morning.

"Oh, the wise men, so-called, would and will condemn me as a fool, a crazy old man who makes up foolish stories. They will continue their singsong chanting voice pictures of things they've never seen or tasted; telling (in all seriousness) of the edge of world's beginnings, balancing their terror of the unknown against the visions of the one they call first dreamer. In vocalizing past visions they place themselves beneath the leafy compost of reality—fertile, but futile at best. They would deny (and truly believe the denial) that the edge of world's beginning was merely where the campfire light merged with darkness. They it was, their grandfathers, who stood or sat in circle, studying the warmth of fire, never daring to turn and face outward to the real warmth of the whole Creation of which they were so small a portion.

"And as for the other they call 'visioner,' a young fellow he was, very serious, everything had to have profound meaning to him. Made himself a stone pipe, and would sit and rub-polish that pipe while he looked off some place thinking. Rubbed and rubbed that pipe until he was rubbing his own hand. That pipe had just gone and disappeared all away.

"And it was his way to light his pipe whenever he got some kind of answer for himself from himself. And so he dropped a live coal into his cupped hand after filling it with tobacco.

"We heard him yell half way to another camp. Looked at each other, we did, kind of worried. We'd seen and heard him before in his enlightened moments, but this was the most powerful yet. We didn't jump up and run to him but just sat and waited, knowing that those who have visions, enlightenments, if you will, or inspirations—these persons (you can usually spot their smug self-importance) will always run to the crowd to crow their inspired insights. Of course I apologize to Crow for using the phrase, and I probably apologize to 'visioner' too, all of it, of course, being my tired-outness at those who would run about advertizing their unique talents.

"So anyway, now that I've forgotten where I was, or why I was there to begin with, I'll re-emphasize my own profound finding: that, if everybody sits around dreaming, meditating, or having visions, who's gonna go out and gather the firewood and hunt for food and prepare it?

"So, anyway, again, why not just think of all this as the end of a chapter, or section of a larger work-in-progress; words sent out like smoke from the fire? We can put a big oak root on the fire, wrap ourselves in robes and in dreaming and just before we sleep think what self-made beings we are, so able to survive, how important we are in the great scheme of things within the Creation. Aren't we gorgeous?

"And just before sleep, let's not wonder why we wonder: will I wake up this time, or is this it, finally?"
❖

Weaver Spider's Web

Coyote was starving and freezing, and here it was only mid-winter. He'd forgotten to gather firewood and food. He'd planned on singing a very powerful song to make the winter a mild one, easy to live with, but he'd forgotten to sing the song.

The reason he'd forgotten was that he was fascinated by Weaver Spider who'd moved into the entrance of Coyote's roundhouse and, there, had begun to weave the most intricate web imaginable.

Now Weaver Spider knew that Coyote was watching him, and he really showed off. He'd work on a tiny section of web, turning it into miniature landscapes with mountains and plants and creatures running all around. And Coyote just sat there on his butt watching the work in progress and making up little stories to go with each picture.

Yes, Coyote thought, this is very important to watch: I am learning many things in my head.

Weaver Spider was of course doing all this so that Coyote would starve and die. He wanted Coyote's house so he could get married and raise a family. And so he kept weaving to hypnotize Coyote, stopping only to eat an occasional bug. Whenever a bug got stuck in his web, he would sing, "Tee-vee-vee-vee," a song which put the bug to sleep and, so, ready to eat.

"Cousin, you're looking very skinny and sick. And it's sure cold in here!" Said Grey Fox when he stopped by one day. Coyote agreed, but insisted that watching Weaver Spider was very important. "I am becoming much smarter," he said.

Grey Fox watched the weaving, but being a practical person, it didn't much move him. Instead he became suspicious of the spider, convinced that he was up to no good.

Grey Fox felt pity for Coyote and went home to get food and his axe for firewood.

Coyote ate the pinenuts and deer jerky while Grey Fox cut firewood. Then Grey Fox built a warming fire and suggested that maybe Coyote wanted to borrow the axe.

But Coyote just sat there, eating up all the food and saying, "Yes, I am becoming much smarter."

Grey Fox got fed-up with this nonsense. He sang a sleep song and a dream song, and soon Coyote was snoring away.

"Now," Grey Fox said to Weaver Spider, "I know you're up to no good. I want you to pack up and leave right now; if you don't, I'm going to have you for a snack." Weaver Spider got scared and quickly left.

Grey Fox tore away the spider's web and woke Coyote up. Coyote looked at the clear sky where the web had been and saw how beautiful it all was. This new clarity, he assured his cousin, had been brought about from watching the spider. And again he said, "Yes, I am much smarter now."

Grey Fox was angry with Coyote. "I'm going to make you twice as smart!" he said. "I'm going to give you a wife, then you can have children to pass your great wisdom on to." And Grey Fox picked up his axe and cut Coyote in half, from head to asshole. Then he sang a song and brought the halves alive. The better half turned out to be Coyote Woman.

28

"Now you are twice as smart." Said Grey Fox. And Coyote Woman looked all around, then turned to Coyote, "Why don't you go catch some mice for dinner? And while you're out there, cut some firewood, too."

And Coyote went out to do her bidding. After he'd gone, she turned to me and sort of looked me over before saying, "I suppose you think you'll be winning over women with your cute stories, huh? Well, let me tell you, you got a long way to go yet."

❧

Coyote's Song

"Grandfather Coyote, sing us a song."

"Yes, Grandfather, tell us a story."

"How was it when you was little like us, Grandfather?"

Coyote sat down and took his muddy tail between his hands, releasing beads of mud. He picked up a bit of mud and held it close to his eyes. "See, I'm cross-eyed and holding one bead but seeing two because I'm looking so close." He flicked the bead over his shoulder. "Now it is behind me and rolling toward world's end, getting bigger and bigger. My inside eyes can see many more than two." He picked up other beads of mud and began rolling them into a ball.

"It was long before there was a beginning. Half-water-thing was arguing with sky-fish about who had the best swimming place. They always argued about this same thing, but this time they reached a decision: they would trade places and find out for themselves, and so they did.

"Sky-fish swam over to half-water-thing's roundhouse when he got hungry, and the old lady was stirring mush in there and just grabbed sky-fish and threw him in the fire. Her son would be hungry when he returned, she thought, and might like a baked sky-fish.

"Of course the same thing happened to half-water-thing, too." Coyote looked at the children. "They say that's why sky is always in water and water in sky. Still looking for those two that got baked." Coyote looked to the surrounding hills, looked far away. "Maker give our tribe all this land to swim around in. Pretty soon you young ones are gonna be going to different places and learning different things, like them others. Gonna get awful curious, too, and look around in their round-houses. Hope you kids don't get thrown into the fire. Hate to see my grandchildren get baked."

The children were uncomfortable and squirmed around. They didn't like Grandfather to be serious; they liked him better when he teased a little. Little Grandson felt as they did. He grabbed older brother's tail and crouched behind it, pretending to hide from Grandfather. He tried real hard and final-

ly managed to cross his eyes. He tried to imitate Grandfather's
deep voice and very solemnly said, "Don't bake sky-fis, don't
bake sky-fis."

The children laughed at Little Grandson, then laughed
harder when they saw that Grandfather was laughing too. He
looked at Little Grandson. "Oh, yes, you are a coyote, no
doubt," he said. "And now I'll sing you a song if one of you
will get my gourd rattle." And when he took the rattle he began a soft, shushing rhythm. At first he spoke softly to the
rhythm, "Before there was a beginning, there was another be-

ginning to join the old one. Before the sky people there were the spirit people. The spirit poeple dreamed of night and sky, and the dream became real. This is the song:

> *Now   now   now   now*
> *there has been a sleeping,*
> *now   now   now   now*
> *there has been a dreaming,*
> *now   now   now   now*
> *our sleep is of dreaming,*
> *and in our dreaming,*
> *we go back to the spirit,*
> *and we sleep with the spirit,*
> *we go back to the spirit,*
> *and we sleep with the spirit,*
> *now   now   now   now . . .*

And Grandfather Coyote sang this song four times, each time a little softer. And after the fourth time, the children slept. He kept the low shushing of the gourd going, going, as he sat, sat gazing into the fire.

❧

A New Dance

Fox: I don't want to die.

Coyote: Well, not many do.

F: But someday I'm going to die.

C: So's everything else.

F: You mean when I die?

C: Sure. Maybe everything is your dream.

F: You really mean *everything?*

C: Why not? It's your dream, isn't it?

F: So I guess I'd better stay alive a long time, so everything doesn't end, huh?

C: (Musing aloud) I wonder if I'd just disappear if I killed him?

F: (Giving up) And I wonder why I dreamed you so mean? Well, go ahead and kill me. You're gonna anyway.

(So Coyote killed Fox)

C: (Looking around in wonder) Well, I guess he was wrong. But I wonder who is the one carrying everything in a dream? Here comes Grandson. Maybe he knows. Hello, Grandson, how is everything?

G: Grandfather, I've been thinking of dying. Do I have to?

C: Please, Grandson, think of something else. Think of living. Look at Fox over there. He started thinking of dying and just fell over dead.

G: Okay, Grandfather. Let's skin him out and use his hide for a new dance.

C: (Looking at us) And that's how we used to make new dances in the old days . . . sometimes.

❖

Coyote Man and the Young Lady

This young girl was good-looking and worked hard
and had her young man all picked out;
she never looked at that Coyote Man who was
always saying, "Hello there, young lady!"

"Hello yourself," her Closer Aunt told Coyote Man.
"Your thing always red and sticking out there in front
maybe you think it's a digging stick for only
using to get all those tender young plants."

Coyote Man, he stooped over and studied the ground
in front of Closer Aunt, "Well, would you look
at those!" and of course Closer Aunt stooped
and Coyote Man ran behind and stuck it all the way,

and in and out Coyote Man was really going
and even up and over once or twice and in and out,
and Closer Aunt said, "yes," she stooped farther over,
"yes, I can see those much better now, yes."

and of course the Closer Aunt was making all this
time pass, so that young girl could be grinding
all that acorn and talking through the knothole
to her lover, making all those plans that they do

about how the lover would come there later on
and they'd fuck through this same knothole,
but all the same Coyote Man so busy, but
sends his ears as birds to listen to the lovers,

then puts a big branch up into Closer Aunt and
hangs a big rock on her back and, "don't you move
until you feel my burning inside of you,
then you must run about yelling, 'it's done, it's done!' "

and Coyote Man runs around the house to catch
the young lover, a man known for his love of gambling,
and by then Coyote Man is kneeling there throwing
his eyes out over the ground and saying, "I won! I won!"

"what, what, how can you win, and how do you play?"
the young lover asked Coyote Man, and he
only said, "huh! you young people don't even know
the good old games we used to play for days,

and days it sometimes lasted, and O, what winnings,
and all the young girls admire a man who wins
and all you have to do is cast your eyes along
the ground and wait for them to click together

and sometimes they click many times, and all these
win counters, though you must be very patient,
and the longer you wait the more clicks you hear,"
so the young lover let Coyote Man take out his eyeballs.

and the young girl was all nervous and kept looking
and looking at the knothole until she finally
saw the big red thing stick through, and she
put herself on it, and at the same time pretended

to be reaching way up to get something, and
up and down, up and down she was going real steady,
and feeling pretty damn good, too, was Coyote Man,
even when the sun had set and getting to be colder

outside where he was standing against the house,
but quickly got too cold and so he reached for wood
to build a small fire as his teeth began to
chatter, and he didn't even know that the wood

was the same one that was in Closer Aunt, and
when the fire reached her tailbone she began
yelling, "It's done, it's done!" and the young lover
heard Coyote Man's teeth clicking many times,

began yelling, "I won, I won!" and the young girl
hearing all this and feeling pretty good going up and
down, she cried, "me too, me too, it's done, I won!"
but Coyote Man, he was already far away.

❖

Coyote Flies

Coyote was watching Eagle flying so high above the earth. I must fly like that, too, Coyote decided. So he went to find the Magpie people, who owed him a favor for his having helped them in another story. He told them about his wanting to fly and asked each for some feathers. He quickly filled his burden basket. As he was leaving their camp, the Magpie headman warned Coyote not to try flying too high right away, "better start in short, hopping flights," he said. Coyote agreed of course.

Coyote climbed the highest mountain around, stopping only to gather pitch. He was thinking how much bigger he was than the Magpies; surely a person so big should fly very, very high, he reasoned.

When he reached the mountain top, he began sticking the feathers all over himself with pitch. He decided that the long, beautiful feathers would make a good-looking headdress, in case he met some show-off bluejay, so he stuck the long tail feathers on his head, between his ears.

He spread his wings and ran and jumped off the mountain. Ass first, he fell and fell, the tail feathers on his head shooting him straight down. He hit the rocks below and skin, bones, sinew and feathers flew scattering in all directions.

Buzzard's family thought he was becoming crazy when he described the big magpie he'd just eaten.

The snows came to cover the scattered bones, and with the snows came tiny iceworms. During the big freeze, these iceworms feasted by drilling holes in Coyote's bones.

And when spring came, the warm winds blew through the iceworm holes, and the creatures heard many flutes and whistles. The creatures came to collect these instruments, gifts of the iceworms. So it was that Coyote's bones were scattered to the directions.

By the time Coyote's brother, Hawk, had finally figured out what had happened and came to put Coyote back together, all he could find was Coyote's dried, shriveled-up anus. So he had to put Coyote back together with this.

And of course, Coyote's been an asshole ever since.

Coyote's Acceptance Speech
After Having Won the Smoked Salmon Award for Humming, from the Downriver People

"Hmmm, mmm, mmm, mmm. Hmmm na, hmmm na, hmmm na, hmmm na. Hmmm . . .

"Oh, yes, there are cords of thought stretched inside the skull. Loosely coiled, hanging slack, damp with grey-jellied boredom, sticky in some if not most persons; the whole of the secret is the simple ability to stretch these cords taut with a power thought. Think strongly and then more strongly, and soon these cords will begin to vibrate inside your head until the sound begins seeping from your nose holes, and soon your entire body will be vibrating from the hum.

"It helps, of course, if a good friend is sitting close by, playing softly on an elderberry flute.

"The hum in each of us is part of our reality. Like the dream, it is a very important element in our lives. Oh, everyone thinks their reality is much more important than anyone else's. But our realities don't have to dance together, and when we meet we don't have to ask, how's your reality? Know it or not, realities merge of their own accord, fade in and out of each other. That's why we have dreams. Dreams are memories of many realities we encounter everyday, and some encountered in the before life.

"Hmmm, naaa. Hmmm . . .

"Yes, even now while humming I was given a dream to happen. It has to do with making love, even though I wasn't even thinking about such things. But because it just came to me, I will tell you of it. She was somewhere close by. A very good-looking woman who has a big abalone disc which she decided not to wear today. And as I hummed, she was following me to my camp. She's been dreaming about love, too, lately. She just remembered the talk about Coyote and how he found a power to make love for days and days without stopping. And that's why she's going to follow me.

"Well, I guess I shouldn't have mentioned that, but the dream was too strong to keep to myself.

"But anyway, like I was telling of how humming and reality are a sharing kind of thing. I feel that strongly. And that's why I'm going to share this big salmon with all of you. As soon as I get back to my camp and that young woman gets there, we're going to eat this salmon with our eyes closed, thinking so hard about all of you that you'll be sharing without even realizing it. No, don't thank me."

Coyote Gives Birth

Yes, he was so hungry, he just swallowed Mole, his own friend, without even chewing. And Mole, he was pretty mad for a while. But Coyote always eats lots of grass and berries, and so Mole was doing all right in Coyote's stomach. And what with sharing all the food every time Coyote tried to take a break or sleep, Mole started scratching Coyote's innards for more food.

And some people think that's why Coyote's always crying about being hungry.

Of course, in another story it was Gopher who got swallowed, and Gopher, he was really mad and right away started chewing his way out.

And Coyote, he was pretty shook up by the pains and by the swelling. Can it be, he wondered, that me, a male Coyote, is giving birth? And sure enough, out came Gopher, all wet and sticky, and looking pretty ugly showing his teeth.

And Coyote looked at those teeth, and oh no, he said to himself, ain't no way I'm going to nurse that ugly baby. So Coyote ran away.

And Gopher, he's still laughing and showing his teeth.

❖

Coyote Man and Saucy Duckfeather

of course they called her that because
of the way she moved her rump to some
secret music or itch, so proud she was,
married to White Crane Man whose every

feather was valued by those over-the-
water-people, sure she was pretty
and even the old men who helped gather
firewood, you seen them eyeing that tail

with their mouths like wrinkled holes,
and Young Singer, too, would hang around
the village and trip over everything
while pretending not to watch her:

yes, all the men and boys of age were
walking around on three legs and not
much fishing or hunting getting done,
not to mention some pretty jealous

women, like Bullhead Woman who took
some old duck feathers and stuck them up
her butt, and wiggle-walked all over camp,
saying loud, "how you like this, huh,

it look sassy enough for all you men?"
but Saucy Duckfeather wouldn't notice
any of these things, down by the shore
she was smoothing her feathers and

looking at herself in the water, and
wishing her secret longing that her
feathers might turn shiny white, and
then, what a gorgeous creature she

would become, a truly fitting
companion for the White Crane Man,
oh, what a pair like sunlight they
would be, and their children surely

shame the great swan so white: and
Magpie Woman was hopping all around
camp, picking up twigs for her
small campfire, and worried, too,

old woman that she was,
with no more men whose duty
was to give her meat of the hunt
and once in a while load of branches,

stirring her tiny basket of mush,
mumbling to herself these last
few weeks, and now, suddenly
reached her decision, and a very

hard one to reach, too, but
nothing else to be done, no,
it had to be, to call in that
crazy Coyote Man, so full of

tricks and mischief all the time and
never content to only gamble
with the men, but had to be
out in the brush chasing after

all those young women, and
now Magpie Woman sighed, and then
giggled in remembering her youth,
yes, yes, there always seemed to be

eager young women, way out
there, pretending to gather wood
or dig for food, the better to be
caught by Coyote Man or any other

like himself, for of course
there are many kinds of coyote,
among all men, not to mention
certain kinds of women, too,

who glory in mischief and hidden
games, among the bushes or in
the forest, but that's always
been so, sighed Magpie Woman

and giggled again in rememberance,
and "yes," she re-decided, "I will invite
Coyote Man to feast with me,
though I have little enough, but

little enough is often plenty for
those whose hunger is not always
stomach food," and anyway she'd
seen that Coyote Man often, yes,

when he'd come to doctor someone,
looking, studying that Saucy
Duckfeather and more, too, in his
eyes than just curious sparkles:

and so, pretending to be very sick she tore
her hair and cried that only Coyote Man
could cure her, and of course he heard
of it soon enough and was seen coming

down the hill with his basket on
his back and singing loud and long a
song which the young men envied
for it could not be imitated because

the hearer forgot it as soon as hearing
it, and only remembered the beauty of it, and
"oh, oh, here he comes again, and watch
out for everything you own and

especially watch out for wives,
daughters, nieces and any grandmothers,"
they said, and Coyote Man he
step-danced into camp and threw

his basket down, heavy with rocks
he pretended were beads, and right on
the foot of Badger's Son who screamed
in pain and danced around on the other

foot, and Coyote Man turned and looked
shocked, and studied the young man's
step, then declared, "well, it's a
fancy step all right, but I don't

think you'll win any girls with
it," which set the other men to
laughing, which good mood Coyote
Man needed to get about his business:

so he took up his basket and went to
the house of Magpie Woman and entered and
stood looking down at her for a long
time, then said, "well, well, yes I can see

that you're not sick at all and will
probably outlive youngsters," and smiled
at her and she smiled back, "you
look just like your father, you

surely do, and wherever did he go to?"
Coyote Man still smiling, "yes,
that old man left for upriver some
time back and I guess he found

a good place to be," and of course it was
the very same Coyote Man because
in old age a coyote often gets
much younger, but secrets are to

keep and so, he asked her what her
problem was and she, she talked
while stirring him a basket of
mush and fed him the last of the

salmon, and he listened and nodded and
mumbled, "hmmm, yes, I see; I got
lots of other important things to do,
but my father was your friend, so

I guess I can help you, yes, I
guess I'll do this thing just
for old times' sake, yes," and he
ate and had a nap to refresh his

mind and dreamed just the right
dream: so when Magpie Woman walked
from her house at sundown all cured, the
camp had a dance to celebrate this

miraculous cure by Coyote Man, and
the feet stomped all night and lots
of rustling and giggling in the
brush after Coyote Man hinted

to certain young women of
the power root he had obtained in
downriver country, which the women
there all used to be sure to have

male children, and this root was only
to be used at night of course and
attached to the front of a man
who knew the song that went with

it: and so Coyote Man slept all the
next day almost, and then faded
into the woods with some of
the salmon and beads brought to him by

grateful young women who were sure
now of male children, and Coyote
Man, when out of sight picked vines
and stripped the bark, and bent them

just like strings of moneybeads, for
of course he had only one real string
for his last night's work, and he filled
his burden basket with the vines

and placed the beads on top, and went
walking fast through the camp and
mumbling to himself so that all
could hear, "oh, these heavy beads

again, and I suppose there'll be more
there tomorrow night that I'll
have to carry away, oh, if I could
just give them all away instead," and

he threw the string of real beads to
some young men hanging around Saucy
Duckfeather, and kept right on going,
and next morning they saw him again,

walking real fast through the camp with
a basket full of salmon which
was really dyed pieces of bark
with a few real salmon on top

which he threw to the people
and mumbled that he wished he
could rest awhile and not have
to be always getting beads and

salmon and taking them from one
place to another, and the salmon
he threw landed pretty close
to Saucy Duckfeather, and so

she began to wonder about this
Coyote Man with so much wealth and
the only one around with no time
to look at her, and there he went,

disappearing into the brush, and then
again in the afternoon he re-appeared, and
this time he was carrying a great bundle
of white deer skins, but moving so fast

that the people could just make out
the one which hung loose, and he
once again disappeared until almost
dark, when he danced into camp,

his head and shoulders turned a
brilliant gold like the sun,
the brightest and most beautiful of
feathers ever seen around, and

eyes of greed, or wonder, or just
dreaming never know the truth of
pine pitch and yellow ocher and quick
motion in fading light: and now,

waiting, waiting, the snare was
set and the prey was curious, as
Saucy Duckfeather began, but
not to let anyone notice, of course,

following Coyote Man around and
he pretended not to notice her and
walked away from camp and looked
to the hills from which he'd come, and

holding his head as in great pain, he
moaned, "oh, I wish that tree would
just leave me alone, oh, where can
a simple man like myself find a

mate for the male tree? oh, I
know it's said that she'll appear
soon, and every wish of hers be granted,
but how will I know her to be

the one the male tree wishes and
how will I be able to tell that
she deserves to be the one? oh,
now that I'm wealthy and have

wished myself a hood and mantle
of golden feathers, still the
other tree cries out to me and
makes my head feel so much

pain, oh, I got to find that
woman for the male tree," and
Saucy Duckfeather did not even
hesitate, but said, "it's me,

the male tree has called me, and
I'm instructed to ask of you,
Coyote Man, what I must do
to have my wish of feathers white

as polished shell or snow, what
must I do?" and he jumped at
her voice, a man caught guilty
and looked at her a long while, yes,

thinking just, oh yes, and "yes,"
he said, "perhaps you are the
one, and I guess I must tell you
the all of it so simple, merely

a tree, a male tree, a dead oak
with a protruding red branch near
the bottom which a woman must
mount and ride upon a four night

ride, an all night ride with
no time wasted, just riding and
wishing a four night journey
to bring about the truth of all

your dreams": and there was Coyote
Man standing inside the hollow oak,
his pecker sticking way out and
so hard his hide was stretched

toward the root of his manhood
that he couldn't even blink his eyes,
and she, the Saucy Duckfeather riding
and riding the magic branch and even,

it became obvious that she was
enjoying the ride: and Coyote Man
blew white ash through a knothole,
and what with her sweat and imagination

and secret longing, she just knew
she was turning white, and being
ridden four nights steady, Coyote
Man was content to leave and

left, and she, poor Saucy Duckfeather was
left with knowledge of her greed and
the acceptance of her given life
with her greyish, long-tailed children,

and old Magpie Woman stirred her
salmon soup and to the idle or curious
would only say, "well, that's the way
of doctors, especially if they're coyote."
❖

Frybread Story

Coyote was making frybread dough
when young Magpie stopped in
to offer his own recipe.

An extra handful of flour and
another dash of salt, he said,
would assure very fine results.

Coyote chased him away, shouting,
"I'm not making very fine results,
    you asshole,
I'm making frybread!"
❖

Rattlesnake

Before he got that name he was known as the Beaded-one because of the beautiful designs which covered his back.

Well, one time he got this terrible toothache, or teethache, because there was a toothache on either side of his jaw. He'd slept too close to ground surface last winter, and the iceworms had found him and drilled holes in his long teeth. The teeth filled with his pain, becoming poison.

He didn't want to lose his long teeth, so he went to Coyote and asked him to do something. So Coyote sewed a tiny pouch behind each tooth to contain the poison, and to also hold the pain. And when the Beaded-one went hunting, he found that his poisoned teeth really helped: just a little bite would paralyze his dinner, then he could take his time eating.

He grew very fat. He grew so fat that he could no longer catch food or even enter his winter lodge. He went to Coyote with his new problem. Coyote said he didn't know what to do about it. Coyote said, "Let's sing, and maybe the answer will come to us."

Coyote took his water drum, then he handed the Beaded-one a rattle. The Beaded-one took the rattle in his mouth and they began. But of course the Beaded-one couldn't sing with a rattle in his mouth. So they sat there looking at one another.

Coyote Woman was stirring a basket of acorn mush. She was listening to the men singing. She didn't think much of the Beaded-one's mumbling song, so she took some sinew and tied the rattle to the end of his tail. Now he could sing. And the rattle sounded pretty good, too.

Coyote stopped drumming to listen to the rattle. Yes, he thought, this is the way it will always be. Then he hummed a power song to make the rattle grow on the Beaded-one's tail. "Well," he said, pleased with himself, "there you are. Now you are Rattlesnake and must warn the creatures when you are hunting, to give them a chance, and to keep you from getting too fat. Yes, I'm sure glad I thought of that."

Rattlesnake was very happy. He became a great singer.

"Yes," Coyote said to Coyote Woman a little later, " I think I did pretty good that time, don't you?"

She was busy at the fire and didn't answer. It didn't matter anyway because Coyote was lost in pleasant thoughts of himself.

❧

Snout

When Snout was a baby he was quite young,
they say, and would cry himself from tit to tit
as if sure while on one that the other was sweeter
and of course never did gain much weight,

and as he grew older all his waking moments
were spent running from place to place
as if in search of something, and his sleeping
was a tossing and turning of face-makings

and mumblings, and upon listening close to
these nighttime mutterings, his mother heard
over and over again, "there must be a better way,"
and so began his early years in search of truths

someone, he was sure, kept hidden from him.
"Bullhead Woman," he said one day to his aunt,
"if your stone mortar was bigger and your pestle
a large circular stone hung from a tree which you

could rotate with ease, why think of all
the acorn you could grind," and she
replied that, "yes, nephew, and if acorns
were as big as coyote gourds we could pick

the winter's supply in one day; and nephew,
have you not heard the grinder's song without
which the oak trees might decide not to produce
at all?" but Snout was already heading for

somewhere else, feeling quite happy that he'd
done his best to help his aunt, and stopped
to listen to Story Teller, surrounded by children
listening to the traditional wisdoms. Soon hopping

from foot to foot in agitation, Snout was telling
Story Teller of the necessity of shortening
and revising all the stories and furthermores,
as the elder sadly shook his head. Then Snout

was gone again and very soon explaining in a
knowing manner to Sandalmaker the lasting qualities
inevitable, if sandals were made of oak, or even stone
and, "yes, and I might use the wood left out of

smokeholes," said Sandalmaker in a serious manner,
meanwhile and patiently, Snout's father, Roundhouse-
builder, was teaching his son the arts of building, and
hoping that Snout would come to realize and respect

the gentle roundness of all things. And Snout
became a very good builder for a while, and
his services were requested even as far away
as up-river country. And the young women, too,

were after Snout in flirting manner, for he
was a man now, and a man needs a wife, and
Snout settled down to building the roundness for
three seasons before he once again started hopping,

from foot to foot in agitation, then, in an ecstasy of
self-gratification, built a house with sharp
corners and shelves and secret storage boxes;
and shocked at last beyond comprehension, the

people watched and talked among themselves, and
maybe, it was suggested, Snout had caught a
coyote flea when he was born and each time
the flea feasted it sucked the brain marrow

from Snout, thus making it inevitable that he
lose for a while his thinking fluids. And, "yes,
I guess we'll have to call in Coyote Man,"
conceded Snout's father at last, "when drastic

measures are needed we must summon a man
whose measures are drastically known," and, "yes,"
whispered Saucy Duckfeather back of the crowd
holding her coyote child close, "bring in Coyote and

let the fun begin," and soon, dancing sideways and
shuffling like a fool, Coyote Man was the center of
attention as he stooped to examine the ground,
and soon a crowd was stooping over the same spot

as Coyote Man suddenly straightened up and,
"hah! I knew it!" and studied the ground
some more, "yes, it was right there before, but now
it's gone, as you can all see," and ignoring any

questions, turned to Roundhouse-builder, "oh, I
know all about your son, Snout, and his sharp
corners; don't forget that even a great doctor like
myself sleeps nose to ass in circle," and he

gave Bullhead Woman a friendly pat on the butt,
and whispered to that old and ugly creature, "it's
just because of you that I come down here, and tonight
you and me's gonna wrassle til sun up," and she

giggled with pleasure, ignoring the knowledge of her
young daughters and nieces. And Coyote Man ate and
slept and dreamed and planned and walked about
muttering in his sacred manner, and made his

plans to cure Snout of his sharp corners and
nosy delvings into other people's lives, and
chose Bullhead's daughter Trout Girl for his
helper, and instructed her, mostly at night, for

many days and reasons. Then Trout Girl followed
Snout around, praising and agreeing with his
many schemes and dreams, and morning often found
these two together whispering beneath a robe,

and the roundness of all things soon included
Trout Girl's belly, and Snout so secure in her
praises gladly paid the bride price and went
back to building traditional houses for the goods

necessary to establish a family. And many children
were born to them, and she, to keep Snout's schemes
in balance, would paint his little plans on pieces
of bark and place them on the fire; and both would

watch the smoke rise, and Snout would smile
contentedly, knowing that his plans were being
kept by the Star People. And the tribe, too, was
content that Snout was once more of the roundness,

and though his plans are still like slivers of obsidian
sharp, sent skyward as smoke they no longer harm
the people, and one man's sharpness is as nothing
when others of his kind live in a roundness.

❖

Spotted Lizard

Very close to the beginning of everything Yellow Lizard was walking across the desert when he saw Coyote. Coyote was walking in a big circle looking constantly at the sky.

"Coyote, why do you keep looking up at the sky?"

"Oh, I'm waiting for the first rain," Coyote answered. "They say that pretty soon water is going to fall from the sky in big drops and make all the desert green with new life."

"Maybe if we stompdance we can make it happen sooner, huh?"

Coyote agreed and they began singing and stomping the ground very hard. A nearby volcano responded to their dance by spewing-up a great cloud of burning embers. Coyote hid beneath a stone overhang. Yellow Lizard just stood there, waiting to enjoy the rain. Instead the embers burned spots all over his body. He rolled in the sand in pain.

"Well, I guess it isn't time for the rain yet." Coyote said, then he did a double-take, looking at his friend. "Hey," he said, "who painted you? You are really good-looking now, with all those spots."

Spotted Lizard studied his reflection in a polished obsidian mirror, turning this way and that way. "Yes," he agreed, "I certainly look better now." Then he looked at Coyote's ragged, summer fur and said, "You know, you could use a few spots yourself . . . or something. You look kind of shabby."

"Yes, well, I dreamed I had a new shiny coat of fur. I'll get it everytime you take a long sleep. So I guess you'll never get to see it."

"Ah, Coyote," said Spotted Lizard, "I think you're just jealous."

Jackrabbit's Daughters

Coyote was bragging himself all over camp. He'd just gotten here, uninvited, to gamble. He'd heard about this big time away downriver, so here he was.

He was losing because he kept thinking about and looking at the women. He wanted a woman and was trying to win one by bragging about his love powers to everyone. "Yes," he was telling them all, "I can keep it hard even when I'm running a footrace.

"Why, one time me and Pelican Woman was going at it so good on a rock that we didn't even notice when we fell into the lake and went right to the bottom. We were going so fast that we heated up the water and it all turned to clouds, and by the time we finished the first round, we were on dry ground. Yes, this thing of mine stays stiff as a walking stick all the time."

"And the second time around there was so much sweat, I bet," teased Old Frog Woman, "that you two great lovers made a new lake, huh? And did you make the salt flats up north when you dried up the sweat the third time around?"

"Seems to me like you must have been watching." Coyote teased back, "I hope you had someone along to keep you happy so you didn't go and get jealous."

"Hah!" Old Frog Woman countered, "Why, Coyote, in my day I could wear a young fellow like you out before I even got started!"

"Hey, hey! Listen to that woman!" Said Old Mudhen, "Sounds to me like she's ready to run out in the brush right now! Better watch yourself, Coyote."

"Well, if she does," Said Old Frog Man, "it'll come as a very big surprise to me!"

"Anything coming from you at all would sure be a surprise. But I couldn't imagine it being a big one!" Old Frog Woman replied, and everyone laughed.

As usual, Coyote had gotten everyone laughing and joking. Everyone was happy now, except Jackrabbit Man. He was sort of listening, but his eyes were on the gambling sticks. He was losing badly. He had a big family and another on the way, and he'd planned on winning some wealth to trade for food. It seemed to him that he spent all of his time out gathering food. And his sons were pretty lazy, spending all their time just playing around. And his daughters, two of them especially, so beautiful and yet no young men came around wanting to marry them.

He looked at Coyote and began to wonder, and to wonder some more. Now there was a young man who might make a good husband for his daughters. He had fancy clothes and carried a burden basket which must be full of wealth. He didn't seem to mind that he was losing, so that must mean he was wealthy enough not to worry about such things.

"You still losing?" Joked Coyote to Jackrabbit Man. "Your concentration must be traveling around somewhere, perhaps it will come back soon."

"Yes," said Jackrabbit Man, "It's just that I keep worrying about my beautiful daughters. Those young men from all over keep sneaking around my place, trying to get to them. And those daughters of mine are such fine basketmakers and always busy making fine, beaded clothes, that I don't want them running-off getting married!"

Badger Man was listening and quickly caught on. "Yes," he told Coyote, "I been in love with those daughters of his all this season, but he won't let me marry them. And everyone knows what a great hunter I am. I would provide for a family very well. But no, Jackrabbit just keeps those daughters of his by his roundhouse all the time."

Coyote studied Jackrabbit and was pretty sure he knew what was going on. "I'd be willing," he told him, "to give you a concentration gambling song, if you'd be willing for me to meet your daughters. I been needing some good baskets for trade and maybe a new dancing outfit. Maybe those daughters of yours could make those things for me in exchange for the song."

And so Coyote taught Jackrabbit the song, and soon he had won back all that he'd lost and much more, and was very happy as he and Coyote filled burden baskets and carrying nets with all the wealth. And soon they were on their way to Jackrabbit's roundhouse. "Remember," he told Coyote, "To speak very softly to them, as they are very sensitive young women."

And Coyote fell immediately in love when he saw the daughters, and settled right down to live at this place while they worked on his baskets and clothes.

"And what's this?" They asked days later, while measuring Coyote for leggings, "What's this hard thing hanging down by your leg?"

"That," he told them, very seriously, "is my curing staff. It is very powerful, and only I can use it. It is for curing many things, especially stomach aches, so if either of you ever gets sick, you must let me know." And as he said this he sprinkled a stomach ache powder into their food.

And so when they came to him with their complaints later that evening, Coyote spent the night curing one, then the other. And both agreed that, yes, it was a very nice-feeling way of being cured.

And Coyote slept between the rabbit daughters, very content. And dawn found Jackrabbit Man standing before his roundhouse entrance, thumping his announcement staff on a hollow log and shouting for all the neighbors to come and witness the marriage of his daughters. And the neighbors crowded eagerly into the roundhouse to see for themselves the new son-in-law. And when the proud father pulled back the robe, there lay his smiling asleep daughters, and between them lay a log with a single, slim branch sticking from it.

"What's going on?" This voice was very loud and seemed to come from the bark ceiling. Everyone looked up, and there was Coyote, looking down thru the smokehole. He was frowning and seemed very disappointed as he said, "So, your lovely daughters have gone and married that log, huh? And to think that I was planning on marrying them myself. Well, if that's the way it happens," Coyote said, climbing down the ladder and beginning to gather up his belongings, "then I guess it happens just that way." He took up his burden basket and walking stick and went over to the log. He poked at the log and said, "I sure hope this fellow is a good hunter. Seems to me that both these young women are going to have big stomachs pretty soon." He poked the log again, "Hey, wake up!" When there was no response, Coyote turned to the people, "He sure sleeps sound, don't he? Guess he's tired-out after a long night."

Then Coyote quickly said his farewells and headed upstream, reaching into his sash for his elderberry flute. And even when he was out of sight, the quavering, mellow notes of the flute could still be heard.

"Well," said Old Mudhen to anyone who cared to listen, "that's Coyote for you. Just when you think you got him in sight, all that's really there is a sound going somewhere else."

❖

The Battle

They were so angry that they decided to have a battle. So terrible was their anger that they would not wait, but declared that the fight must be fought now, immediately, on this very spot. Fox blamed what he considered to be the crime on Badger. Badger in turn was all for placing the blame on Cougar.

Jackrabbit hopped in agitation, calling for Mole and for Mouse, and for Deer and Bear to fetch their sharpest arrows and their heaviest warclubs.

By the time Coyote arrived the sides had already been chosen, the battle lines formed, and the smell of hate and future bloodshed permeated the very air.

He, Coyote, listened to all the threats and promises of broken bodies to be. He walked out and stood between the enemies, declaring very solemnly, and in a very soft voice:

"No, I cannot allow this great fight to happen just yet. There has been no battle-preparation dance. There has been no pipe of cleansing. No, the Creation does not wish this battle to take place just yet."

And some say it was Bear, but strangely, no one actually remembers just who it was. Bear denied the accusation, but someone ran from one of the lines and struck Coyote dead!

And Coyote fell and indeed lay there, very dead. And the cry for immediate battle was resumed, and the menacing cries for blood again filled the air,

when, from the opposite end of the battle lines, Coyote again stepped out, dancing and brandishing a huge club.

He ran to his dead self and struck a tremendous blow upon the body, then turned to face the creatures, shouting: "Who killed this person? Who struck him down before I did? Was that person purified? Did he sweat himself and think of the children? Did he dance to assure that the life cycle continue?"

"Enough talking!" someone shouted and ran to Coyote and struck him dead.

And again, much later, no one remembered who or what struck the blow which killed Coyote for the second time.

Then from the left hand side of center, Coyote ran out swinging a great club and struck at his fallen selves until all that remained were two masses of fur and blood and broken bones and twisted sinew.

Then Coyote danced the dance of victory over his own fallen selves, pledging their death to his own great anger. Oh, he danced, he really danced.

"Now then," said Porcupine, "how is it that this one who dances the victory in battle dance, when it was not himself who killed himselves? Is it within reason for him to claim this doubtful victory?"

"If I did not kill these two, then who did kill them?" demanded Coyote. "Let him step forward to claim these deaths, that I may kill him too in revenge."

When no one stepped forward, Coyote declared, motioning to his dead selves, "Then obviously, these kills are mine!"

"It seems to me," began Elk, who was interrupted by Skunk, who also began, "It's quite obvious to me that . . . " "Now hold on a moment," said Badger. And Coyote wheeled on Badger, shouting, "Hah! Don't you know that you can't hold onto a moment, let alone a minute?"

And so they argued, all the animal creatures, about the finer points of who might or might not claim a kill.

And the women of these great warriors, at the urging of Coyote, prepared a great feast, so that these mighty warrior-debators might continue on full stomachs.

And soon, the recent anger was set aside for the more important battle of words leading to reason.

And by this time, everyone having forgotten all about Coyote,

he, Coyote, took his fallen selves by their tails and dragged them away uphill.

Then he took a good hot sweat bath and then sang a song of renewal known only to himself, and soon his other selves revived. "Now," said one of them, "that's what I'd call making your point the hard way. You know, it really hurt when you killed me."

"Yes," said the other self, standing up and stretching, "the next time this happens, don't forget it'll be your turn to be killed."

"Hey, maybe this won't ever happen again, huh?"

"Oh, it will happen again." Coyote said, "Yes, it always seems to happen again."

Then he merged into himselves and walked away, far away.

❖

Drum

Badger's Son went to Coyote's winter camp
Where Coyote spent his days and many nights
fashioning drums which were able
    to make very beautiful songs.
"Coyote Old Man, will you teach me
to make those drums that only you can make?"
    asked Badger's Son.
"And what, nephew, will your first song
be about?" And Badger's Son said,
"Why of course it will be about you."
"Nephew, I'm very sorry, but, I've
just forgotten how drums are made,"
    answered Coyote.
And Badger's Son walked slowly, sadly home,
hurt, but not angry. And waited four days,
    and again went to Coyote's camp.
"Coyote Old Man, I must learn to make
those drums that only you can make;
and my first song will be
a thanks to deer for his skin."
Coyote shook his head sadly, "Nephew,
I surely wish I could remember how
to make those drums, so I could teach you."
So Badger's Son left Coyote's camp,
and decided to have a long sweat bath
    and clear his mind of making drums.

On the fourth day of his sweat, he saw a drum,
floating before him, making sounds
    like tapping raindrops.
He followed his vision, and bent a frame
of cedar to a roundness. Now I must
    get some deer hide for the head, he thought.
Then he picked up a stick and pretended
to beat a gentle rhythm on the empty drum.

He imagined a song.
The song was about the Creation.
All things around him grew silent,
        listening to the song.

Coyote Old Man quietly entered the camp
and sat and listened until the song was done.
        "Nephew," he said, "you have indeed become
a very good drum maker."
Then Badger's Son handed Coyote Old Man
the headless drum, and he, Coyote,
        began to drum and sing.

And all the creatures entered camp
and began to do a round dance.
        "And where," asked someone,
"did such a fine drum come from?"
And Badger's Son said, "Oh, it was
Coyote Old Man who refused to teach me
        to make this fine drum."

❖

Coyote Did Not Want
to Create People

Coyote carried a burden basket
of dreams
dreams woven of willow and the smoke
of ashes
ashes long asleep upon a sloping
ridge
of ribs which were the dried skeleton
of a promise
cried against the night moon wind
of a storm
which cracked the husk of a sleeping
season.

He said to us:
  I was a past poem recited in
the shadowed circle of your campfire
do you recall the dreams I lent you
walking thru childhood
and didn't we together sew a fringe
of sharpened edges like the shell
of snapping turtle?
      Why then
do you clutch today like a lidded
box hiding your very own secret,
didn't you swallow the bite of wind
I sent to rock your cradle board
on the flute of oak branch
where hung your newborn breath?
  Here, sit down, take this handful
of corn meal and feed the universe.
  I will tell you a story:
Long before I was born I once
hunted upon a mesa which stood
on clouds. I was cold and I rubbed

my hind legs together trying
to make First Fire. A cricket
fell from my anus chirping. It was
so dark a night that the sun laughed.
Just before dawn an unseen creature
of huge wings enveloped everything.
I began crying and crying. My tears
became a stream which made a lake.
A loon laughed at me. I made a
shelter of abalone and turquoise,
then sat and cried somemore. My
crying turned to coughing. I choked
and spat-out black obsidian.
The night ate it, so I swallowed
the cricket. The taste was so sweet
that my stomach became many poems.

These I chanted all around, but
nothing listened.
    I dreamed of wings.
I rubbed my hind legs together.
I became grasshopper chewing
tobacco and spitting out honey.
A tree frog fell from my anus chirping.
    I grew afraid, and as soon as I
did, fear was born. I swallowed
it whole and warts broke out
all over my body. They chirped
and jumped from me on strange feet.
    I was the beginning, yes, I was
my own dreaming. I rubbed my
hind legs together again. A bird
flew from my anus chirping.
    I stopped. I was afraid.
I did not want to create people.
When you appeared, I cried.
I fear you.
        That's all.
That's the end of this story.
❧

He was sitting by his campfire, listening to the star echoes.
His burden basket rested upright against a pine.
    The voices inside the basket got pretty loud and disturbed
Coyote.
    He struck his head inside the basket and said, "You
people be more quiet or I'm going to dump you out all over
the world."
    They didn't make another sound for many, many etern-
ities.
❧

Coyote Makes the First People

Coyote stopped to drink at a big lake and saw his reflection. "Now there's a really good-looking coyote," he said, leaning farther over.

And of course he fell in. And of course you will think this is a take-off on an old theme.

But what happened was, he drank up the whole lake to keep from drowning. And because he didn't really like the taste of certain fish, he spat them out. And because he felt sorry when he saw them flopping around, he sang a song to give them legs.

"Maybe they'll become the first people," Coyote mused aloud.

"Oh, no you don't," said the headman of that tribe of fish, "if it's all the same with you, could you just put us back where we were? And could you please take away these stupid legs?"

So Coyote regurgitated the lake and put everything back the way it was.

Again he saw his reflection and said, "Okay, you're pretty good-looking, but are you smart? I've been trying to make the first people for a long time now, but nothing wants to be people. So, what do I do, huh, can you tell me?"

His reflection studied him for a long time, then it squatted and dropped a big turd.

"Okay," said Coyote, "I guess that's as good an answer as any."

Then he himself squatted, and began to fashion the first people.

❖

Those People Will Believe Anything

"Let me introduce myself, Coyote."

"Well, I've heard it all now. Imagine, a turd on the trail talking to me."

"Don't call me a turd! My name is Harvey!"

"My old woman, she aint gonna believe this. A turd named Harvey?"

"As a matter of fact it was you who dropped me here last week."

"Hah! I got you there! I didn't pass here last week. Besides, my turds don't have names, and, they don't talk!"

"Well, maybe it was your grandfather. I just figured I had to start talking sometime."

"Well, I'll tell you something. There are people living around here. If I was you, I'd keep quiet.

Cause those people will believe anything."

❖

"Oh, yes, I made the first people, but I didn't really, because I was different then. Well, what I mean is like this pinenut." Coyote paused to fish a pinenut from his pocket, held it up between thumb and finger. "Yes, like this pinenut. It was part of the big tree, then fell off, then got picked up, then maybe was eaten, or took seed." He squeezed thumb and finger together, then opened them quickly, and no more pinenut. "Or maybe it never was even there or here." His nieces and nephews sat around him wide-eyed, waiting for the next wonder and storing away the words and especially the actions for later.

"Yes, I made the first people out of dog shit because it was nice and warm and not too sticky, even though there weren't any dogs yet." His sister was looking from the kitchen and frowned at this, then shrugged, knowing it was useless to interfere. "Dog sit?" asked a little boy. "Yes, that's it for sure, dog sit. So I made the first people out of dog sit, and they was just little kids sitting around in a circle and thought I was their uncle, but you can always tell from their smell what they're made of." Coyote frowned around the circle and sniffed as at something with a bad odor. He looked pointedly at his little nephew, then went and opened the door, still looking at little nephew. The boy giggled and said, "Oh, no, no dog sit, no, no."

Ignoring the children, pretending he'd forgotten them completely, Coyote walked out into the yard and looked around. The children followed their uncle and watched him expectantly. He whirled toward them suddenly. "What? What was that you said?" The children looked at one another, confused, knowing that they had not spoken. Coyote looked down at the ground, did a doubletake, then knelt down to speak to an ant. "Well, well, I didn't know you were here!" He looked at the children. "Why didn't you kids tell me that Little Cousin was visiting?" They crowded around him to look at the ant. "Do it talk?" asked little niece. "Sure he talks," said Coyote, motioning to the ant. "Me and Little Cousin here used to spear salmon together back home in up-river country. Course that was before they made him little."

It was a-little-bigger nephew's turn to bite. "How he get little, Uncle 'Yote?"

"Oh, it just happened the way it usually happens," Coyote said, talking like everyone should know this fact. "Yes, we was cooking salmon in camp, and this family of ants, they had a roundhouse across the river, and it was their territory we were in, so they come across the river on oak leaves to claim their share of our catch, only Little Cousin didn't know about this, 'cause he was raised in town like some other people I know are." Coyote was sharpening a little stick as he spoke. "Anyway, Little Cousin got mad at those ants for getting into the salmon and started stomping them. It was terrible, all that yelling and screaming." The children were shocked, remembering stompings of their own with guilt. "So Little Cousin got turned into an ant so he could learn what it was like to be one, and if he don't get stomped himself I guess someday he'll get big again."

Coyote put his ear close to the ant. "What? Oh, sure I'll tell them," he said to ant, then turned to the children. "Says he'd like for you kids to leave him a few crumbs of bread once in a while, but not too much or he'll forget to try and get big again. What I'll do is, I'll stand this stick here in the ground, and when Little Cousin got his underground roundhouse filled with enough crumbs, he'll take this stick down to let you know he don't need any more."

The children stepped carefully, following Coyote back to the house. He went into the kitchen and sat at the table. He pretended to ignore the children and told his sister, "Them little ants out in the yard invited me to a round dance tonight, so if I'm not here in the morning I'll probably be down there." He turned to the kids. "Maybe you kids can holler down the ant hole every once in a while so I don't stay down there too long. Those ant dances usually last quite a while or so."

"Two days and already got the itch, huh?" his sister asked.

"Oh, no, nothing like that. Just got a little business to take care of. Be back around here before you know it."

His sister pretended anger. "Little Coyote business, if I know you. Well, just don't ask me to be bailing you out of anything next time."

Coyote tilted his chair and eyed the children. They eyed him back, waiting.
❖

76

Why, Coyote, Why?

Because the stars are a round dance
and we are of the earth lodge,
out through the smokehole into night
the warmth of our bodies and our cries go
the fire of wood is bones and sinew
to the thought formed in dreaming
in once upon a season into season,

because Creation laughed once before
tears of rage tore minds the roots
of calm waters into storm
and blood on hands sticky
reflect the thinking's hunger
to crawl broken and alone
in crowded towns and cities
with eyes closed upon mind
upon reason, forgotten,

because a child is born wanting
and parents are milk and warmth
of the sleeping seed of the thigh
of the marrow bone ribbed sky
lost creatures all, calling Creation
to witness a smallest thought,

because I call nightly the moon
and you shiver in your sleep who
should join me haunch to haunch
howling eager head back proudly
a wanting chorus the universe
awaits contact be it truth
or merely contemplation,

because a mind of stone unturned
is winding into a core of crystal
which will shatter the very stars,

because I offer you vast stores
of food grown in the mind of Creation
and you eat instead the cold ashes
of an abandoned fire, and clothe
yourselves in where you think
you might be going,

and because I am the shadow
of your wants which you ignore
and turn your eyes inward
in self-pity and constant doubt
while a feast sits waiting
so close you have but to reach,
but reach instead neatly formulated
conclusions based upon your doubt
to boost your withered ego
to the level of mental ankles,

and because my throat grows parched
in trying to sip your futile thoughts
and my body and mind grow weary
awaiting your image to reflect
itself on the underbelly of reality,
     that's why!

A Few Passings

It is cold and damp and stars seek to enter his eyes like slivers of pain. The root of an oak is pressing into his shoulders. He lies in a shallow pit, not knowing how he got here.

Well, I must get up now, he thinks. He cannot move. There are strange sounds within his head, like bursting light. Now there is a frightful wailing close by, a high-pitched cry. Where did he hear it before? Yes, of course, it is his sister, keening. But why does she keen?

Now I must get up, he thinks again, it is too cold here and I might get sick. But his body will not move.

A handful of dirt falls upon his feet. He recognizes the deep voice of Uncle. Hey, what is this? he wonders. Another handful of dirt falls on him. I'll scream, that's what I'll do, he shouts in his head.

I am being buried! There is no feeling, only a sensing of things. There is the memory of a blinding light and a great impact.

The dirt trickles into the cavity of his chest, where his ribs, spine and all those muscles and sinews have been torn out. When was that?

He can't blow off the dirt falling on his face. No more voices now, instead a thud-thudding of heavy stones, a grating click of stone on stone.

No, he thinks, the creatures will not reach me for a feast. I would taste sour and mean, anyway, he thinks, giggling inside his head.

He rises slowly and in silence above his body, floating there, looking at his sister and Uncle.

They think I am dead now, they really do. Maybe I should touch them and let them know I am still here.

That's how I told myself it happened. I really believed it for a while.

It's so strange, this floating forever, this entering and passing through other floatings, other forms that once were living meat.

Now I float into new places, into total darkness which is true light. I separate, by thinking, into many floatings.

"Go back and tell them, why don't you?" What a strange idea. Where did it come from?

I am of this tide, this floating and drifting, this gentle rocking. I laugh bubbles and pollen, wisps of rainbow gases. I caress myself with thoughts which are an ecstasy.

I have always done this, eternally.

The other coyote hide, thrown over the barbed wire fence next to his, snorts a slight contempt at his words. Then they remain quiet for many days, their hides growing stiff and dry, until finally, the other asks: Hey, you awake?

Yes, I'm awake. How can I rest with these maggots eating my tailbone? You know, I never knew that they hum while chewing, or maybe it's grumbling to one another.

Yeah, I know what you mean. That ugly cowboy sure didn't skin us out good. Thought he was gonna puke, too. Guess we smell pretty bad to him. Course he eats the same kinds of food we do, and some others even us coyotes wouldn't touch. But I wish he'd scraped off the fat so we didn't have these maggots.

Yes, it's kind of uncomfortable. I feel like I want to scratch and can't . . . Umm . . . Wonder where he threw our carcasses? You'd think we'd be able to feel where they are; after all, our brains are wherever they are.

Hah! Let's not try to figure that one out. We might find out just how much those brains of ours were really worth.

It's funny, though, isn't it, that we can still think inside these empty hides.

They thought about this and other things for many, many days.

One day a dog passes, pauses, sniffs, and eyes the hides. He looks around to be sure no one is watching, then bristles and growls at the hides. He's getting ready to prove his bravery by attacking a hide, when the hide suddenly growls.

The dog lets out a yelp and is gone, tail between legs, far across the field yelping.

They laugh and laugh themselves into choking.

Hey, how did you do that?

I don't really know; just by thinking it, I guess. Kind of like when we found out a while back that we could see through our eye holes if we wanted to. When I saw that dog and figured his plans, I just kind of got my maggots together and made them growl like me.

And it worked!

I stretch myself; I spread; I tighten
into a long, taut tension of vibrating sinew;
a quivering. I'd studied the star path
and willed my mind in climbing upward
I was stretched between here and there.
Coyote Old Man was balanced at my center
jumping up and down, twanging the string of myself.
He was laughing at me; hey, he said,
you're a real coyote all right;
can't make up your mind where
you really want to be.
Hey, my young friend, let go at one end
or the other and let yourself snap together.
Should I do it?
     Do what?

His hand on the doorknob, hesitating:
now what the hell's wrong?
He goes back, to stand in front of the mirror.
He raises his hands and looks at them
as he would at strange, unknown creatures.
I won't look into the mirror, he thinks,
I know that those eyes are watching me,
waiting for me to look up.
I'll just leave this room before it's too late.
But he looks up at the face in the mirror.
The eyes are downcast, looking at strange hands
which are not reflected.
The eyes in the mirror slowly
rise to meet his own.
The faces smile at each other, embarrassed.
We better do things together, he thinks,
as he turns and leaves the room abruptly.

The eyes in the mirror turn to watch his departure.
They seem confused.
The head bends and the eyes, again downcast,
     study strange hands.

❖

Island

I dreamed Coyote was running around and around my house. I sat up and looked out the window, and sure enough, there he was, going round and round.

Faster and faster he went, creating a dust cloud. And when the dust settled at last, my house was surrounded by a wide, deep canyon.

Then it rained for many days. And I was an island.

This thought went out to the surrounding trees, and they whispered, "He is an island."

I shook the woman sleeping by my side, and told her, "Look, we are an island."

"No," she said, as she packed her belongings, "we are never an island."

She walked away from me, crossing the water as if it were dry earth.

I stood at the edge of the canyon and watched as it became an ocean.

I tossed and turned in my sleep. I reached for the woman sleeping by my side. She was gone.

Then I reached to wipe away my own tears.

Nothing was there.

Nothing.

Black Coyote

He was called Snowfox-running
of that large but scattered tribe
which hunted the frozen plains
and endless lakes of the far country,
born within the wail of a blizzard
his muzzle whiskered in frost
he whimpered an unknown hunger
his mother's milk could not quench.

He became a skilled hunter, and
even when very young often led
special hunting parties in the season
of the howling wind of hunger,
well respected by his people, he
had gained his hunting powers
by thinking hard and dreaming
himself to the places of food.

> It was a song brought to him
> on the wind of ice-breaking
> which gave him strange powers
> to see into the beyond;

> "I am given to sing it once,
> and then three times more,
> that I am to be a shadow
> cast upon unknown stone."

And his tribe and family wept
when he prepared to journey
for they thought he spoke of death
and would see them no more,
and he left a faint trail, soon
covered by snow, and was gone
crossing many plains and mountains
to the land of sage and sand.

He searched for and found the singular
circle of Coyote Old Man's sleep
and sat respectfully to await
the old man's own time,
and Coyote Old Man studied him
frowning at what was to be
having seen the whole process
in his lately dreaming sleep.

> "And so you are here and I
> am to ask what it is you seek
> and you will answer that you
> think you must become a shadow,
>
> and I must begin a ritual new
> to my mind's knowledge, and
> disagreeable to my thinking
> but I am Coyote, and will
> anyway."

And Coyote Old Man built a fire
of sage and juniper in the sand
beneath the sky singing softly
feeding the fire slowly, slowly,
plucking out glowing coals
and blowing and talking to each
then setting them to rest on sand
to let them blacken and cool.

And all the while he ground the
charcoal, he spoke of and pointed
to moon shadows close and far
saying, "These you will become,
part of but separate, merging
like day into night, season
into season, back and
forth a running rhythm:

> now, as I rub you with charcoal
> now, as I rub-in shadow pigment
> now, I take away your voice
> now, I take away your body,

you are a no one now,
you are a nothing, lost
like the memory of loneliness
the echo of a keening voice.

Now that you are nameless you
must follow me closely, making
every gesture I make and even
echoing my inner thoughts,
now when moon her fullness
lends us light, you are a motion
only, a shadow truly, moving
slowly across the cool night sand.

Nameless, you follow me and
become my footsteps, my
hind leg twitching in sleep, yes
you now enter my dreaming,
become as one with my ears
and nose, and soon you see
from my eyes and think
you think from my mind.

 Yes, you are a shadow now
 yes, as one with that which
 is me we run barking,
     look
 now I will give you a dance,
 a moon dance, take it, it
 is yours, and
     look
 now I will give you a song
 take that, too, and sing:

and watch me as you sing as I
tear you from me
    see? Now you
I tear you from me laughing
yes, I am laughing now,
you are brother to me now
not blood of blood so much
as shadow of shadow, echo
of further echo, see?

You are a shadow cast in stone
and bigger in body than I
and your voice will also be
a more penetrating voice,
but your steps will not be seen
for even a solid shadow leaves
no trail, and you will travel
only at night, forever, at night.

> And you will turn the humans
> sleeping, with your voice, and
> they will worry in their dreams
> and wonder, and create a dance,

> and form a Coyote Clan of
> hunters and scouts, and all
> because they heard your voice
> and let it tell them what

they wished to think they heard.
And I will answer your keening
voice from the opposite hill
and though we never meet again,
we will sing together even until
the last human may perish
from having forgotten to dream
for the benefit of tomorrow.

And now I loose you wholly
and, see, now you have a shadow
of your own, to lead or follow
through the seasons' cycles,
and I name you
                Black Coyote,
dancer and singer of shadows,
disturber of human dreaming.
Go, the seasons await you!"
✦

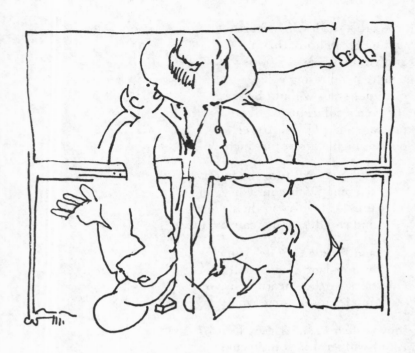

As I Sit Here
Writing Down His Words,

a dark wind is blowing rain against the windows. Oak leaves
tap. I put more wood on the fire and turn to see my eyes reflected on the window, for outside is blackest night.

When the wind stops for a moment I realize that coyotes
are barking and keening very close. I open the door to listen
and hear a moaning like that of a wolf. But wolves have not
walked these hills for many years.

Again that moaning, and the hairs on my neck tingle. It
is my imagination, of course, I tell myself. I am seeing a figure
in my mind, but no, for it is there. A ragged human wearing
an old army longcoat, long hair plastered down by the rain
upon his face, but not bothering to brush it from his eyes. He

is out there in the wet and darkness, stumbling around, slowly, from tree to tree to rock outcropping. He searches the ground with frantic eyes and those eyes and his mind are the only quick movements. He drags his walking stick behind him, now stumbling to another dark shape just ahead of him.

He is sobbing now as he realizes he may never find those he seeks. They should be camped right near here, but there are no signs of a fire. Wasn't it just yesterday that they . . . but no, it was much longer. He moans again low from deep in his chest and stumbles toward another dark shape.

The coyotes are all around him, watching and wondering and wanting in some way to help. The younger ones begin a yapping, hoping the others will join in. They falter and stop. A young pup is so agitated that he begins circling like a dog, biting at his tail. The oldest of the pack sits and watches the human.

The human rests on a slight rise, sitting with knees pulled up and arms folded over them, hands hanging limply. Water is pouring down his face, rain and tears. He stares at the ground before him as if emptied now of all emotion.

The oldest coyote studies the human for a while, then raises his head and begins a few deep, starting barks. He looks at the human and repeats the barks.

The human slowly raises his head to listen. Then he raises his head further back and from very deep within begins a low wolf moaning, and then the others join the song.

The human's eyes are closed and head still back, and rain and tears stream down his face.

❖

For Rattlesnake:
A Dialogue of Creatures

(Each speaker is introduced by a voice)

snow plant, child of winter:
> see now the curving browness emerging from snow
> as earth her winter robe begins to fold,
> a trickle of moisture
> a gurgle then sand
> > rolling,
> so like a pebble-filled gourd
> clasped between hands
> to mute to gentle murmur.
> then freshets sigh the hillsides
> and stones to roundness tumble
> > > > their praise.

cedar, oldest of trees:
> yes, my friend,
> and dawn breezes lend me voice
> my branches whisper
> and sweet
> > my scent
> mingles your own breath
> as we await the others.

woodpecker:
> it seems then a short night and day
> that berries sweet have mantled
> the mountain's greenness,
> then bear-who-used-to-be, would . . .
> (a long pause)

oak tree:
> yes, brothers and sisters.
> bear, no more his soft and heavy walk
> bear, no more
> > his strange and sacred manner,

flicker: (quickly)
    are we about to speak of THEM
                      again?

fox: (as a chanting)
    I remember the last of bear's tribe
                    dragged
      by fear-sweating horse
    foaming from whip and smell
      eyes rolling   and bear
    great clots of blood

    and the human   a most awful smell
      of hate
    and fear and lust
    and the thought-pictures
                of his mind
      hurting all,
    and we wondered at such cruelty
    for his thought-pictures
      were of himself
              torn and devoured
    by others of his likeness.

squirrel:
    wasn't this get together supposed to be for rattlesnake?
    hey, coyote, what of you,
    your silence is like a burr
      beneath my tail.

coyote: (man in old long coat, floppy hat, long tail he strokes)
    yes, well,
    rattlesnake is on his way and should be here soon.
    and don't forget
               it's said
    that we are here to stay
    as long as one of us remains,
               and . . .

bluejay: (interrupting)
    who said that?

coyote: (innocently)
    why, I guess I just did.

lizard: (stamping his foot in agitation)
    you know, this is beginning to sound like
    a made-up lie and the liar
    don't know what to say next.

a voice: (of rattlesnake)
    I am a manner
              a custom
     a tribal creature.

coyote:
    he's here!

rattlesnake: (emerging from concealment, carrying his head)
    I come to you cut in half
    and cut again   headless
    with strong heart beating a constant pulse
    I crawl to you bloody
     a nightmare   of man's genius

    I too am springtime
    like my brother bear
    for together   we emerge
    from sleep
    to the dancers pounding feet
     and the wormwood smell.
    I rattle them a music of my nearness
    but they fear my dance
    and axe, or knife, or gun, is the feast
     I am given.

    I tell again of the creation
    and beg the peace of their council
    and name the many clans and tribes
     that none be omitted.

I teach them the necessary lesson
of alertness
of mind and body ever ready
for the tribal will
   but
they have forgotten the allness
   of the creation
in their eager quest of vanity.

I lie headless and bloody at their feet
   who am
   their former brother.
(begins to chant)
   I dream bear
   I vision bear
   I call bear
      we must all become bear.

bear: (a dark mass, slowly shuffling in dance, four times in
       circle, slowly, humming, as to himself, then pauses to
       speak)
       they kill my body
           they
       skin me and leave my body
           as in shame,
       let us
             then
       begin again the praise
       forgotten by man.
       snow plant, please begin again.

snow plant, child of winter:
       see now the curving browness emerging from snow
       as earth her winter robe begins to fold,
       a trickle of moisture
       a gurgle   then   sand
            rolling
       so like a pebble-filled gourd
       clasped between hands
       to mute to gentle murmur.

       then freshets sigh the hillsides
       and stones to roundness tumble
                                    their praise.

cedar, oldest of trees:
       yes, my friend,
       and dawn breeze lends me voice
       and my branches whisper
       a weeping as from an evil dream
       of creatures born of hate

       let us again
                  then
       chant the evil back
       into earth's womb
       to be reborn
                    or not
       as will be.

all the voices:
    Man no more
      look
    he is fading,
    man no more
      see
    he lies in dreaming,
    man no more
      forever
    let us forget the pain,
    man no more
      forever
    his bones of dust
    the wind is taking
      to scatter
              to scatter
                    to scatter,
                        to scatter.

❧

Cut-Outs

When you see me step-dance sideways
grinning wicked, laughing, joking,
don't take me for a sample of
what you sometimes want to be:

I use a parchment of dried seaweed
and a piece of sharp obsidian
to cut you out holding hands
in an endless row of yourselves
with a grin hole at one end
and an asshole at the other,
and no matter from what angle
or direction I approach you,
you look about the same:

once upon a river floating
belly-up I was dreaming
that I was singing very loud
and woke myself up and now
I can't get back to sleep:

hi hi hi ho, hi hi hi ho,
ho ho ho hi,
            ho hi, ho hi;
and that's how easy it is
to make up a song:

did you know that I can digest
just about anything; a stone,
a feather, a five-dimension thought?
yes, just about anything except
that question mark after *thought:*

when I build a roundhouse,
I always work in a circle:

see these pebbles and this sand?
was once a fine river, until
you drank it, then stank it
out of existence,
and now you can only see it
on very hot days
dancing above its former self:

once upon a city sitting
at world's end above
the salt water sandstone,
a flight of gulls dropped
whitely, like shadow-echoes
upon the dancing waters:

sitting once upon a city
above world's end on sandstone
water salt a dropped gull's
flight echoes whitely shadow-
like waters dancing upon:

so I take the parchment cut-outs of
all the *you's* and paste them up
on the wall of the world and
hopefully, you will be able
(and even want to)
to tear yourselves loose
into someplaces.

❧

Hump-Back Flute Player

us:
All thought and eyes and wanting fingers
were given the flute
        and fascination
the antennae
                quivering
so like a trembling question
        and the eyes
                    O, those eyes
a gentle deer
                wary
graceful,
        and to others
                    a bug
beetle upright walker
                    loner
        rock to rock
lost to us in space/time
found by us and placed
        in dreaming.

Cast in stone and in silver
    still vibrating
jade-tipped antennae
    obsidian eyes
          reflecting
our own loved eyes
and holding back a smile
    behind flute
        a note
a sharp crystal ringing
    an inner
        penetrating to
mind drum,
cast in stone and in silver
    pendants of thought
become grandfather
loner lurking
      between shadows.

we:
Resting easily
    relaxed
hump to rock to ground
    note to sky
        flute
us, we . . .
    (Stop!
for just now above clouds
beneath feet feeling
      thunder
    sky darkens
crouch to paper pencil
    hunch-shouldered
    await rain
      darker still
and thunder directly overhead
    and now the huge
    spatters of rain
into heavy falling early afternoon
    darkness
      and shivered

        just now
at cracking thunder sudden
                        overhead
rain heavier
        and wind
leaves pulled from trees
        fern and sumac
        dancing shivering
corrugated roof next door
each rib a runoff river
        waterfalling
                to instant pools,
grasses bowed to ground
lakes and swamps,
                then
        as suddenly gone
        into dry earth.
So back to)

we:
Resting easily
                relaxed
hump to rock to ground
        note to sky
                flute
us, we, all the they's
        that we are
making cute obstacles
we prefer to call
                art
        dazzled
                by our own
talent.
        Pause here.
Reconsider
        the hump,
and think myself back
to a sweat lodge.
        Goodbye, we, us,
                for now.
Hump is emptiness blackness

voidness spaceness
        overflowing
                    pouring outness
blackness,
it is rattle and waterdrum
                        hump
        is bottom of well
        is earth core
womb of creation
                    is skin
                    is membrane
is pulse container volcano
nova black hole in space
        space is
                space is
vacuum sucker tidal pull
        is hump of flute player
in skidrow merica street
five gallon tin tied to back
        filled with nothing,
collector of dreams unwanted,
little packets of nightmares
        tiny packets of fear
        of hate
                    of wanting
tiny bundles
                tied neatly
        with sinew
and tied here and there
all over his body
his skin pierced neatly
        (he never even bleeds).

again, all:
the note of flute
                        loneliness
memory   meat
to none
        self-pity   tragedy.
The hump is the gourd
        is the vessel

102

is the awakeness
to awake and rub hump to rock
feel feet on ground root
                    tendrils
        wanting permanence
and find instead
                    a doubt
again
        of self.

(Coyote was fastened to the very ground
by rawhide thongs and driven stakes:
        well, he thought,
                        well, well.
Yes, I am staked down to the very ground,
        well, well, he thought,
standing there looking down
at himself
            for you see
Coyote is of magic, thought Coyote,
and further thought to pity
this writer of fantasy,
well, Coyote thought again,
if he can't think beyond words,
        that's too bad,
                        I guess,
though I don't really give a shit.)

we:
Taking note of sound
        with pencil,
        I end this particular
                        piece
and strip naked to enter river
        river endless
        river constant
        river forever
                    part
        of the cycle
I dive into
        your current.
                        Onen

Discarded Scene

They'd just finished dinner. Coyote was full. He helped gather the dishes, and as he did so, his host suggested that he put on a record.

"Here, let me!" Coyote said, grabbing a greasy dinner plate. He went and put it on the turntable.

From a far away somewhere, at some time, a low sound, a sort of a moaning was heard. As the sound approached, it became that of a cow herd moving slowly across a prairie.

Smoke, and the odors of cooking meat began to come from the speakers. There was the sound of a shot, and then silence.

"That wasn't very good." Coyote remarked. "Let's try the flip side." And when he did so, there was a great roaring laughter from the platter itself, and a voice which bellowed: "Flip side! Side flip! Back flip!"

And Coyote began doing back flips all around the room, unable to stop.

His host gently closed the door to the room in which Coyote was caught. Then the host began doing a slow waltz, hugging himself, humming with his eyes shut, vaguely smiling.

The scene faded and all that remained was a backdrop of slowly falling stars.

❖

An Arrangement

Three dried stems of grass. A horizontally branching twig of bittersweet. A single, tiny, hand-like bit of cedar bough found upon the ground.

How to place their stems within the narrow neck of a delicate, ceramic vessel?

Ah, good . . . But no, perhaps I should break one of the grass stems, to give a sharp downward angle, to balance the bittersweet.

But that's manipulation, isn't it? Well, so's picking them in the first place.

"We're out of kindling." Coyote Woman said.

Hm, cedar kindling sure makes a nice, smooth, splintering, creaking, tearing-like-jerky noise as the axe penetrates. If I close my eyes I can daydream the sound into scenes and sensations and imagine all kinds of . . .

Yes, Coyote is even like this, sometimes.

❖

Relativity

"Coyote, do you understand the theory of relativity?"

"Yes, yes, I do. It's much easier that way. When I'm hungry I just stop at anyone's place and get a meal. Yes, it's really good to know that all creatures are related."

❖

It was another beautiful day, and Coyote was thinking that next time maybe it should be raining and cold. High on a rounded, grassy hill overlooking assorted cities, sipping mellow wine and wind with some young students. His mole was resting a few feet away, head covered by a leaf to protect its weak eyes.

"Hey, how about Alcatraz, huh? I mean, like how did it all come about?" This from a softly bearded youngster.

Half-dozing now, eyes shut upon a bright red moving behind eyelids, Coyote nodding to himself and registering a question. "Yes, that. It was probably the barbed wire. Hard to know where to start, it was.

"Old Uncle, now, he owned one of the few treaty tents left over from the U.S. Surplus sale in the early 1800's. Used to explain to us youngsters how the treaties wasn't broken, but more like torn, tattered and scattered around. Collected all these old Indian treaties and patched the holes in his tent with them. Some big museums offered good, hard cash for that tent, but the old boy was kinda sentimental about it and wouldn't let it go. Remember he used to sit inside on his robe and poke his fingers through the bullet holes. When he went, his family burned it up for his journey, 'cause no telling how long he'd be on his way on that sky trail, what with all his cattle rustling and womanizing. Family claims there's a whole tribe of Little Uncles down south a couple mountains over.

"But what it was, we was bull rabbit hunting that day and figured to use the old pitfall-surround and stampede system. Kinda scared we was, not wanting any serious injury, and everybody sort of sticking close to each other, but casual-like.

"We was going along pretty good, close to the fence to try to keep them from tearing it down and getting away. I don't know; gopher hole, rock, or maybe a loose piece of wire, then horse down and me flying through the air and end up wrestling a twenty-foot section of fence, barbs biting here and there and one tearing into my shin bone like to pull it loose. I scrabble-crawled to the downed horse, smart enough that horse not to move, had his eyes closed and his front hooves crossed over his head for protection. I just got down behind that old boy and stayed down, too, could feel the air whistling over my head whenever they jumped over.

"When it was done with there were bodies all over the field, downed horses screaming. Lucky nobody was serious hurt. Indian Agent and his patrol come out there in a heli-

copter to negotiate with us to confine our activities to within reservation boundaries. We kinda agreed but wouldn't sign no papers. Cousin of mine once signed a government windfall check for another guy and ended up doing three to five, so we wasn't having none of that.

"Wound on my shin didn't never heal properly. Lucky my other leg never got a scratch." Coyote rolled up his pant leg and examined his shin. The students crowded around to look. Coyote examined his shin a bit. "No, sir, not a scratch on this one." He closed his eyes and lay back in the grass. The students _____ and then _____.

Mole came over and climbed up Coyote's shirt and across his neck to bed down in his hair. "Louse," Coyote mumbled, as he fell asleep.

❧

Coyote's View

"What's your view of things, Coyote?"

"Well, it mostly depends on how I'm looking at them, I guess. The angle of perception is important, too, of course. And the whether or not of open or closed eyes and mind.

"All in all, I'd say I tend to view things thru my crystal. Much more clarity there, and it tends to filter-out misconceptions, too."

"You know what, Coyote? You talk too damned much!"

"Yes, I agree. And you, Asshole, ask too many questions."

❧

Sneeze

Coyote was sneezing and couldn't stop. He'd been down-river to town visiting relatives and had gotten to know some dogs. They were thought to be distant relatives, and so he'd hung around with some of them, ass-smelling and all, like they did. Some pretty crazy goings-on, too, what with male dogs trying to mount other male dogs.

Now, ass-smelling isn't a bad custom, not if it's only an occasional and tentative kind of getting-to-know-one-another thing, but those dogs really carried on. Seemed like they couldn't get along without it and kind of got nervous when there weren't any asses around to sniff at, like maybe it made them insecure, somehow. Well, the young ladies hadn't been too bad, though.

Coyote went out to chop kindling for grandmother so she could start the mush. He was remembering that one big dog who scared all the others with his growling and always wanting to fight. Coyote'd been reading some candy wrappers at the curb and pretending to be so caught-up with interest that he'd ignored that big dog looking for trouble. Just kept reading, he did. So pretty soon that big dog was looking over Coyote's shoulder, trying to see what was so interesting. Then Coyote backed up real quick and bit that dog on the haunch real good, and then Coyote was rolling his eyes and tongue-out growling-mumbling-drooling and slobbering and all, and that big dog took off yelping about Coyote having the hot summer madness. And big dog's owner mad as hell and yelling at big dog, "Get him, boy! Kill him!" So Coyote still acting and slobbering all over the owner's shoes, backed that human right against a wall scared stiff, then calmly pissed on his leg.

Then it was the police and guys with shotguns running all over screaming about mad dogs. And Coyote running, too, puppy-happy, yapping playfully at heels, tail-wagging his butt all over the place and quick out of town.

"Yes," he told grandmother as she served him mush, "yes, we gotta keep away from those dog guys in town. Can't even catch a rabbit, and fall on their faces if they don't got a leash to lean into. Don't watch out, pretty soon they gonna be just like those goofy humans."

Coyote circled four times and curled up into a tight ball beside the fire, nose to ass in circle. Hope my sneeze is gone, better not sneeze, he thought as he dozed off, or I might blow myself inside-out.

Coyote's Broken Tail

Two men carried him by clasping hands to make a seat. It was too painful for him to walk. He heard the old woman's cackling laughter as piercing as a loon. "Oh, now I'm gonna get it," said Coyote. "Oh, that old woman's gonna do me bad for sure."

The old, legless woman was rubbing her hands in anticipation. She cackled again, loud and clear, scaring her grandchildren. No, she couldn't resist and hollered, "Who you men carrying to this old healing woman, huh? What! What! Coyote, did you say? You mean that old nasty who runs after my married daughters and laughs at my warnings? Him, do you mean?" And again the blood-curdling cackle, and the whole village listened from hiding.

Coyote was sweating now with the pain of his broken tail and the further pain he knew was coming.

They were before her house now where she sat upon a blanket, rubbing her hands. "Broke your tail, did you?" she demanded.

"Yes, grandmother, and a very painful hurt it is, too."

"Yes, and only one way to pull that nasty thing back into place," she said, raising a crooked talon. "Maybe should use an old digging stick instead; yes, down through the big mouth and bottomless stomach, ho! But probably lose the stick that way, huh?"

He could offer her strings of beads and meat, but no, it would be useless, he knew.

Bare-assed and all but whimpering, they laid him before her. She'd thought it all over as soon as she'd heard about his broken tail. He was probably expecting a long time of pain, a series of cures to turn his hair white; but . . .

She quickly plunged her middle finger into his ass to the knuckle, then hooked the bent and broken tail bone and yanked it up into place.

And Coyote's howl was like none other ever heard, and the people of the village shuddered.

He lay then, entirely spent, breathing deeply,
waiting,
and realized that it was done,
and finally, and confused,
looked up at the old woman,
and she was grinning through her wrinkles,
and gave him one quick,
knowing wink.

Street Scene

A beautiful, sunny Berkeley day of crowded sidewalks, arts, crafts, street musicians and strolling poetics. A perfect day for magic or madness. Hong Kong silver competing with metal pounded in India, back to back with ceramic flower pots facing a Japenese screen from which hang photographs of naked, meaty limbs. A beautiful gone-gypsy girl dances with swirling skirts and dogs happily bark her flashing ankles. On one corner bluegrass music and across the street a recorder and guitar lie side by side in intermission.

Coyote is leaning against a storefront watching in fascination the customers at a candle penis table. The Louse pokes its head out of the pouch at his belt and looks at him sternly; "I could tell you not to, but you're gonna anyway, aren't you?" Coyote ignores Louse, stuffing it back into the pouch like tamping tobacco. He flips a two-headed mental coin and approaches the seller of candle penises. It's a deal after a short consultation and exchange of money.

It's kind of nice having my own business and all, he thought, leaning back in the chair, his prick protruding thru the hole he'd drilled in the table, throbbing there among the wax impersonations. The young lady was blushing but more confused than angry. She was a swinger, after all, and decided to go along with the joke. Coyote had guided her hand to his prick to guarantee the life-like quality of his wares, "Just feel the warmth and texture of this fine penis! Two dollars and yours to do with as you will." It felt real all right, and was!

"Girls, ladies, step right up and feel these luxury items. A steal, I assure you, at two bucks." She cried, Coyote's self-appointed shill. A few brave women went along with it and felt, then paused in consternation, it was real! Coyote winked and grinned at each in turn and they found themselves smiling back at this ugly creature.

Pretty soon his table was surrounded and he was making change so fast that his manhood was wilting. "Hey, look at this one! It's melting from the sun." Everyone part of the

joking now as one young lady volunteered and proceeded to caress it back into shape.

Coyote was taking names and phone numbers for house calls now. He was the world's greatest wax penis hustler, declared another young lady. Coyote modestly agreed and gazed fondly at his pampered member.

"Perverted filth! Disgusting exhibitionism!" Shouted the middle-aged street preacher, violently sweeping the candles from the table and in the process almost breaking-off Coyote's prick. The crowd began booing and stamping their feet and clapping in time to: "Penis hater! Penis envy! Penis hater! Penis envy!" And here came the blue-helmeted riot squad, pushing the crowd back with their riot sticks.

Coyote stuffed money and phone numbers into his pocket, but the excitement wouldn't allow his prick to soften enough to remove it from the hole in the table. "What the hell is this?" One of the cops demanded of Coyote, getting ready to grab this obvious trouble-making-faggot-militant-son-of-a-bitch.

And three Hare Krishnas never knew what hit them, buried now with full-nirvanic honors after having been struck down in their prime by an insane creature wielding a huge square shield.

And Coyote running, running Coyote, between cars and crowds, penis still thrust forward in blunt confusion, knowing only the basic theory of survival, holding the table in front of him.

Last seen wedging himself and table into a VW bus driven by a grinning young lady.

The street corner philosopher witnessed the whole episode and sipped his coffee between puffs on his pipe, dreamily gazing off into space, preparing a mental thesis based upon a moral ending he was certain he may have witnessed, though the morning paper chose to describe the whole scenario in terms of, "An obvious and vicious militant attempt to rally a march upon the university, and averted only because of the fine performance of Our Tactical Squad!"

And of course, that's enough for any one story.

❧

"Well, I at least crippled that old sonabitch. Maybe even shot his left forefoot off." The ranch foreman ejected the empty shell from the 30-30 and slapped the lever shut on a new round. "Probably bleed to death; if not, I'll sure get him next time." He looked at the Indian. "Yeah, well." He paused. Damn Indian always made him uncomfortable. "Going into town on business. See to the feeding, will you?" Coyote nodded and headed for the barn.

He hooked a bale and dragged it over to the calf lot. He snipped the wires and began pitching the flat squares into the trough. He sat to watch the calves eat and thought about the coyote. He'd seen him a few times, a ragged-looking old timer, always way off, head low and trotting. Now he was shot. According to the rancher and the foreman, that old coyote had been here forever, stealing and sneaking around making their lives miserable.

Coyote went and got another bale. He wondered what they'd think if they knew his real name. Laugh, probably, just laugh.

Owl didn't show up that night, and Coyote was glad. He'd been expecting those heavy flapping wings outside his window. A russle of cottonwood leaves and a *coy-ot, coy-ot* hadn't happened, so he guessed that the old coyote was still alive.

Next morning they were getting ready to hitch the low-bed to the tractor for hauling bales. Coyote was fueling the tractor when he heard the yelling and cursing turn into moaning and almost crying. He ran over to where the foreman sat, his left foot crushed beneath the tongue of the lowbed. Impatient as usual, he'd accidentally knocked the tongue off the block while slamming at a rusted bolt.

Coyote had to use a pole to lever the tongue off the foreman's foot. He drove him into town then, the foreman for once quiet, his face the shade of putty from pain. Coyote knew that some bones had been broken and that the foreman would be in a cast for quite a while.

When the rancher handed him his check next day and mumbled something about, "Not much doing; can't keep you on; maybe next season . . . " Coyote wasn't surprised. No, he assured the rancher, he didn't need a lift into town; he'd walk.

The rancher was sorry to see the Indian go; a good worker, and quiet, not surly like some of them. His foreman had insisted, though, calling from the hospital and bitching about bad luck and trouble-making Indians. Well, he'd wait a few days and then go into town for a new hand.

Coyote headed out across the fields, his pack and bedroll lightly riding his back. Just before he crossed the last fence he saw the fresh droppings and then the tracks of that old coyote. He smiled then and thought he saw a grey motion at the corner of his eye. He didn't turn to look but crawled through the fence.

It wasn't far to town; he'd be there long before dark. He began to trot, head bent slightly forward, his feet padding lightly, nose sucking and releasing air in rhythm to his trot.

Coyote, trotting an irrigation ditch, pacing his run like the seasons. The air was cool, was clear, and there was a happiness in him now, trotting, trotting.

❖

Coyote's Anthro

The anthropologist was very excited. He'd just received his doctorate after having delivered his paper, entitled: The Mythology of Coyote: Trickster, Thief, Fool and World-Maker's Helper. He was at this very moment in the process of gathering further data, working on a generous grant from a well-known Foundation. He'd just set-up camp in the sagebrush not far from his latest informant's shack.

Now he sat by his fire, looking at the stars and sipping coffee. He chuckled to himself when he heard a coyote bark not far away. He wondered what that coyote would think if the myths about him (or her) were read aloud?

"Not much!" Said a voice. The anthro was startled, he hadn't heard anyone approach. "Not much, maybe just a cup of coffee and some of that cake I see sitting there." Then into the campfire light stepped an old man, but not a man. He had long, furry ears sticking thru his felt hat, and he had a long, bushy tail hanging from beneath his greatcoat. He leaned on his walking stick and grinned.

Good God! The anthro was stunned: it was Coyote Old Man himself. But it couldn't be; he was a myth!

"Not always." Coyote said, as the anthro closed his eyes and shook his head violently from side to side. When he opened his eyes, Coyote was leaning toward him, his head cocked sideways, listening. He nodded, "Yes, I heard them there in your head. Sounded like pebbles. Is that how you anthro's make music?"

The anthro knew he must be hallucinating. Better go along with it, he thought frantically, and maybe it'll go away. "Uh, are you Coyote Old Man?" He asked.

"Do I look like Fox Young Man? And do you really want me to go away?" Coyote studied the anthro, then asked, "What time are you?"

The anthro raised his arm to look at his watch, "Well, it's exactly . . . "

Coyote interrupted, "Nothing's exactly. It's not tick-tock time I asked about. I just want to know what time you

are." The anthro looked blank. "I thought so," said Coyote, "Well, let's have that coffee, then we can maybe figure things out."

So they sat drinking coffee, the anthro so excited he couldn't sit still. He reached for his tape recorder, then looked at Coyote, "Uh, do you mind if I turn this on?"

"Why not? Do you pet it or sing to it? Will it dance?"

Once he'd turned on his tape recorder, he felt more confident. He was, after all, an anthropologist. He picked up his note book and pencil, and began, "I'll pay you for your time, of course," he said.

"It's not really mine I'm worried about, it's yours I'm here for. How can you pay me for my time when you don't know what your own is? How about this time? Yes, this time put a little more sugar in my coffee." Coyote laughed at himself, then looked seriously at the anthro; "I'm a doctor, you know. I'm here to help you. Now then, how can I help you?"

"Well, actually, it's the stories I'm most concerned with. The reasons behind the reasons, if you follow me: interrelationships, the problem of spacial paradox, sexual taboos, those kinds of things. I want to creat a whole fabric of thought, a completed tapestry, no loose threads. Know what I mean?"

"Parrot Boxes, huh? Sex shell tables and follow-youse: what's all that? That how you talk about pussy in college? You know, you sound like my tapeworm, and he never did make any sense. How about just one question to begin with, huh?"

"Well, let's start with the Creation myth, cutting to the core! What's the meat of it really, the true meaning?"

"My friend," said Coyote, "If you think Creation's a myth, you just might be in serious trouble. It's not the learning that's important, but the leaning. You must lean toward your questions, your problems; lean slowly so that you don't bend the solution too badly out of shape."

Coyote plucked a long hair from his tail and held it horizontally a foot from the ground. He whispered something to the hair, then let it go, and it floated there where he'd held it. He took a sip of coffee, then placed his cup on the hair. The anthro was incredulous: the cup sat on the hair above the ground. He blurted out, "But how did you do that? What's holding the hair up?"

"You're not studying your notes to this story very well, are you? If you'll just relook at the paragraph in front of this one you'll find that a foot from the ground is holding things up. Of course, you can't see the foot 'cause I just made-up its measured guess. Something invisible is sleeping under this sand and only its foot is sticking out."

And so, because this story is getting too long, Coyote became somewhat impatient, and quickly finished his coffee. He stood up and beckoned the anthro, "Come on then, we got some leaning to do." And Coyote led him across the desert to a deep pool of water near some mountains.

A full moon was reflected in the water, shining as brightly as the one in the sky. Coyote sat down and began singing. Then, still softly singing, he leaned out over the water and touched the reflected moon. The water bent to his touch like rubber. Still singing he stepped onto the water moon, bouncing slightly. He jumped a bit and bounced up and down.

Then he began bouncing in earnest, bounding into the sky, even doing a couple of back flips. He bounced as high as he could and grabbed the moon in the sky and hung there grinning at the anthro. "Hey, look at me," he said, "and I wasn't even sure I could do it."

He let go of the moon, did a double flip, bounced once and landed next to the anthro. "Okay," he said, "I got it all nice and rubbery. Go ahead and bounce a little."

So the anthro jumped from the bank, creating a great splash as he sank from view. He was gasping and spitting out water as he climbed from the pool.

"Well, well, look how you shattered the moon . . . You know, I thought only us coyotes were silly enough to try things we weren't sure of. And you, my friend, forgot to sing."

❧

Short Coyote Story

"Coyote this—Coyote that!
Why do you keep picking on me?"
Coyote complained.

That's all he said, so I wrote it down,
and I guess it's a pretty short
     Coyote story.

❧

Sierra Foothills

deer
a stirring of leaves
I took to be your journey,
or was it the wind?

bluejay
already scolding
as I squat, about to shit,
must you announce all?

        an unsettling incident
this turning insect
who confronts me with feelers
        waving, what to do?

        manzanita
polishing your skin
of red, a misting of dawn
        bids us, awaken.

        kitkitdizze
I saw the hump-back
flute player, sitting beneath
        you, disguised as Ant.

        coyote
all night he's eating
berries, and saying by turd,
        I'm just passing through.

        coyote again
those turds on rock tops
monuments to his humor,
        how does he manage?

        and again
sitting eating grass
chewing it into a mash,
        humming a question.

        or for that matter
he told me for sure
that without my telling tales
        he'd have his, anyway.

❖

Coyote Would A-Hunting Go

Coyote went to England once
on a lecture tour. He talked about
why the ocean separated the
continents and why the English
and other Europeans should
stay where they were.
                              So he got
thrown-out of England and came home.
But while he was in a pub over
there, he learned a hunting song
(The Keeper Would A-hunting Go)
he really liked, so he brought it
home with him for a visit, and
changed the words.
          He called his song: An
Ethnopoetic Experiment In
Ego-Evacuation.
          Here's how it goes.

"Coyote would a-hunting go,
he didn't go fast
and he never went slow,
he was just looking
for a doe, doe, doe,
          in Sierra foothills country.

He stopped to pee up in the snow,
he melted the ice
till it started to flow,
it went to the valley
as you know, know, know,
          and made the Yuba River.

          With a hey, hey, hey!
          may it rain all day.
          Why go out
          if you don't know the way
          in Sierra foothills country.

Coyote was so happy that he cried
he wrapped his teardrops
in a hide,
and threw it on
a mountain side
        and pinenut trees there sprouted.

He cried the manzanita bush
and made the oak trees
with a wish,
filled the lakes
and the rivers with fish,
    in Sierra foothills country.

    With a hey, hey, hey!
    may it rain all day.
    Why go out
    if you don't know the way
    in Sierra foothills country.

He stubbed his toe along the way
got mad and said
someone must pay,
I'll make people
on this day,
    just to confuse each other.

Not satisfied with this fine curse,
he said I think I'll
make something worse,
a creature which speaks
in esoteric verse,
    and so he made a poet.

    With a hey, hey, hey!
    may it rain all day.
    Why go out
    if you don't know the way
    in Sierra foothills country."

Coyote's Discourse on Power, Medicine, and Would-be Shamans

Good evening, friends. You notice this long, straight branch I'm carrying? It's called a ten foot pole. It's best used to approach certain subjects which don't like to be approached. Then, if the subject snaps at you to bite your head off, or your heart out, with a bit of luck it'll bite the pole first and you can run away.

You see this old hat I'm wearing? It smells kind of funky, but it keeps the sun out of my eyes and the rain out of my hair. It also holds my head together, which is why I never take it off. By holding my head together, my brains stay intact. And you'll also, I hope, notice the holes in my hat from which my ears protrude? These ears, of course, are my sensors, used to detect sounds which immediately are fed to my brain for diagnostic purposes, for clarification, if you will. You will also note that my mouth is situated slightly below my ears and brain; and the other object of interest, my heart, is even further removed from the others. When functioning. The progression is from ear to mind to heart, then back to mind to be either stored away for later reference, or from mind to mouth to express an opinion on the information received.

Of course this isn't to say that the other parts of the body are not also vital, for they are, each necessary to the other. Like all things within the Creation, the loss of one causes an imbalance within the whole.

Take an asshole, for instance, that puckered, smirking thing we coyotes refer to as "the other mouth." The upper mouth takes in nourishment and also spew-out words, often incomprehensible. But the lower one knows enough to do only its job, which is getting rid of waste material, or compost, to put it better.

Speaking of assholes, I knew a young fellow once, about one-tenth as smart as he claimed to be. Lost his asshole one time because he forgot to listen. He was out gathering mushrooms when one of them spoke to him and said, "Don't pick

127

me. I am a medicine!" He immediately plucked the mushroom from the ground and popped it into his mouth: figured, hell, if this is medicine maybe it'll do something wonderful and strange for me. (For of course this young fellow was never happy or healthy, being always too busy telling others how to live to take the time to take care of himself). Well, he got really sick. Vomited, farted and shit all over himself. Shit so much, in fact, that his asshole fell off without him even knowing it. Probably still running around looking for it. Yes, he's the first person I ever met with a detachable asshole.

Anyway, I'm here tonight to speak of medicine and those some call shamans. I need the money you're paying to hear about these subjects. So, okay, I just mentioned both in one sentence and that's probably a beginning.

And now I want to tell you about a young woman I met on a famous university campus. Met her at a party. She walked right up to me and started looking at me thru a crystal. She looked and looked, then told me very seriously: "I'm a medicine woman, you know. You must come and see me." I kept a very serious look on my own face and told her solemnly, "Yes, I will come to see you. What is your name and address?" "Oh," she said, hesitating momentarily, "Shamaness Fast-Walker. Meet me by that big oak up the hill. Right after the party." Then she walked away to crystal a few others.

She was pretty good-looking, so I went and met her later. Asked her to put her pouch of crystals behind the oak, then we got down to the business of the two-backed dance and other forms of strenuous frivolity. After our final performance, which was a take-off on aerial acrobatics done hanging from an oak branch, she retrieved her crystals and proceeded to "do me," as she called it. It was a full moon night. The stars glittered and danced within the crystal.

I'd learned very young to counteract powers I had not requested. I stared back at her through the crystal. She began fading. I could see the moon thru her body. Her eyes dimmed and her mouth opened to plead with me. But it was too late. I couldn't stop myself. She faded completely away, not even leaving the trace of a shadow.

Someday I'll bring her back. She did know some good tricks, though they had more to do with body magic.

I went to another party on the same campus, given to celebrate the arrival of a well-known poet. His fame was based on the fact that he was, quote: "A Shaman Poet!" unquote. Now, that's really heavy, I thought, settling down with the others to hear his poems. He began chanting his poems in a deep, slow voice. Every other line spoke of his powers to understand all things within the Creation. His choruses called on his powers to hear him, to reaffirm these powers.

He was beautiful, his long hair swaying in rhythm to his body movements, his white-streaked beard jutting-out in profound wisdom. I was very impressed. I looked around at the others and saw that they were as if in a trance. His words and motions had acted to put everyone under his spell. Oh, he had power all right, real magnetism.

I reached for him with my mind, to share some of that strength. I touched a shell and put my ear to it. I heard the echoes of his own words bouncing back and forth within a hollow shell. Then I probed his mind. I went inside of it to find a tight bundle of self, a bursting ball of energy looking out of eyes which were intent only on seducing his audience.

I felt sad. I withdrew and sat with the others. I'd stopped listening, for I was depressed. Here is no shaman, I thought, here is a powerful mind centered on self.

Being a creature native to this continent, I'm often accused of siding with my indigenous relatives. I deny this and will state at this time that power and wisdom are universal. No one center of this earth possesses the allness of power. I would also like to say at this time that phonies, too, are universal. But then perhaps, like decay, the phonies are necessary compost to the growth of real power. But who can know?

Take a drum and a rattle. Take a people sitting in circle around a fire, singing songs of the Creation. The very same songs their ancestors sang.

Now take the same people and let a flea of dissatisfaction bite one of them. A young man (let's pick on him) takes the drum passed to him by an elder. Even before he consents to begin drumming, he must first change the painted designs on the drum. Then he removes the feathers and replaces them with bells. Now he's ready. He begins the ancient beat, then hesitates. It is too slow. So he speeds up the beat to satisfy and keep pace with his quick mind. The song is new. The people listen respectfully, seeking to share a newness. But the young man is still not satisfied, and before the people can begin to comprehend his song, he has begun another. Then quickly he does variations on the theme until the theme itself has been lost, swallowed-up in his frenzy. Even he has forgotten the original theme. "Well," he says, in explanation, "That's progress!"

Sort of reminds me of a pup when it's agitated for some reason and begins chasing and biting at its own tail. That's what's called "a tight circle of concentration."

Where was I? Seems like I'm going in circles myself, don't it? Do I seem bitter or anything? I hope not, after all, I want you to invite me back.

Yes, well, the first time it happened was so long ago that even I barely remember. It was a girl child out walking thru the forest alone. But not alone, because the little people were curious and followed her. She was out walking because she felt bad. Her father had been hurt while hunting. He'd cut open his leg on a branch sticking from a tree at ground level. He'd been too eager, he admitted to his family. Game was scarce and he was trying too hard and had forgotten caution. It was his own fault, he insisted. And now the cut was swollen with puss and would not heal.

And so the little girl was walking, trying to keep herself from crying. Tears were not much of a cure for physical pain, she knew. The little people sensed her great sorrow and decided to let her see them. They wanted to know why she was feeling such sorrow.

They let themselves be seen by her. She'd always known they lived in these woods, but this was the first time she'd seen them. They were all very formal as they introduced themselves. They liked her very much and felt a deep respect for her sorrow.

130

Asking politely the source of her sorrow, after they got to know her, she told them all. The little people sat with her in silence for a long time. Finally, one of them spoke softly, telling the girl to continue her walk, and to pay close attention to everything she passed.

The girl continued on into the forest, watching and listening. In a clearing, as she stepped across a small brook, she heard a tiny, polite cough. She looked all around, but couldn't find the source. Then the cough was repeated and she looked down. There, right next to her, a small green plant was nodding and moving its leaves. There being no breeze and it being the only thing around in motion, the child knelt to study the plant.

It spoke to her then, apologizing for coughing and inter-rupting her walk. The plant explained that the little people had asked it to help her. It then told her that it possessed a power of curing. It would teach the girl its powers if she would take the time to learn how to use it properly. The pro-cess was involved, but was soon learned by the girl. It in-cluded a cleansing, a chant, a song, a slow process of prepara-tion, a further singing to be shared by the person being cured, and this was to be followed by a thank-you feast for the Cre-ation. The plant emphasized that the thank-you not be made to the plant itself, but to all things within the Creation.

The child picked the plant and some of its relatives as instructed and returned home. She told her family of the gift she'd been given, and then prepared the cure. Her father was cured so quickly that he was able to go out and hunt the very food which was used for the thank-you feast.

The girl child grew to maturity and became known as a curing person. She always followed the first instructions given by the plant, step by step slowly, so that she made no mistake. As she grew in mind and body, so too grew her knowledge of medicine, for the little people never ceased to talk to her even in her old age. And as time passed, she was given to know many other curing plants, one by one as they were needed.

She shared her knowledge with a few others, so that it would stay alive within her tribe. Not everyone is given the patience to learn the curing arts. Many other skills are needed within a tribe to assure survival. Usually, as a person grows, their own particular skills will manifest themselves. As with everything else, when all the arts and skills are combined, a strong unity exists within the tribe.

And with all this I'd like to add that I've never yet met a person of power (except himself, of course) who gives themselves titles such as medicine person, power person, or shaman. Even within a tribe or nation, the people know who to see for their particular needs, so why give them titles?

When porcupine goes night walking, he doesn't look behind himself and say, "Ah, yes, I got my quills with me." He knows what he's got.

Well, my friends, that's about it for this time. As you leave you may notice a little basket sitting by the door. It's called a hunger basket, and if you would be kind enough to feed it a little money, it will be a very happy basket.

Thank you.

❧

Coyote, Coyote, Please Tell Me

What is a shaman?

A shaman I don't know
anything about.
I'm a doctor, myself.
When I use medicine,
it's between me,
my patient,
and the Creation.

      Coyote, Coyote, Please tell me
What is power?

It is said that power
is the ability to start
your chainsaw
with one pull.

      Coyote, Coyote, Please tell me
What is magic?

Magic is the first taste
of ripe strawberries, and
magic is a child dancing
in a summer's rain.

      Coyote, Coyote, please tell me
Why is Creation?

Creation is because I
went to sleep last night
with a full stomach,
and when I woke up
this morning,
everything was here.

Coyote, Coyote, please tell me
Who you belong to?

According to the latest
survey, there are certain
persons who, in poetic
or scholarly guise,
have claimed me like
a conqueror's prize.

Let me just say
once and for all,
just to be done:
Coyote,
he belongs to none.
❧

It's upvalley now, in a ground fog, tires whining the slick pavement, whooshing cars and trucks and headlight traces shooting by. A big bottle of Old Crow and whiskey breath smell mingling damp clothes and gas fumes. The driver is nodding to the talker, and the singer in back is silent. It is like an endless trip across the land, forever dark and damp as the headlights probe and probe. The towns pass by like blinded, crouching creatures, and solitary lampposts cast a yellow halo of loneliness on empty roadways.

A winding road in moonlight with the far down hiss of boulder-tumbled waters. Each pine tree holds a wide-eyed owl, and the crickets have forgotten their songs. A cloud momentarily fades the moon, and Coyote takes another drink, left hand guiding the car, foot to floor in uphill climb. "Well, I don't know . . . it's . . . " He says this as if contemplating an important question, then glances to the seat next to him, then to the back. Both hands are tight on the wheel, and he's trying to figure out where he's left his friends. He's alone and was talking to someone a moment ago. Something has been with him too long now, he thinks, and hears a harsh laughter in his head.

The horse knows the trail, and Coyote dozes in the saddle to awaken to occasional clacks on stone. There's the sound of the river, and just below, the fish camp abandoned before his time. His mind is on the riffle and the boy on boulder, salmon spear poised. The camp laughter and wood smoke and racks of drying fish, kids hauling fallen branches and driftwood for the fire. The boy is gutting a big salmon, and the blood colors the water. The hairs on Coyote's neck tingle, and was it him, the boy, or some other, Older Uncle maybe? The bodies face up and face down in the water, on the boulders, along the bank, clutching scrub brush or empty air, jagged, black-ripped holes in backs and chest. Old Man with head cut off and young girl leg-spread raped bloody. Blood in stream. And the child, young life smashed against

stone, a tattered bundle of twisted cloth. A dry sob chokes
out, and the horse pauses; a slight heel nudge, and it continues.

He's walking the upriver trail and can't remember where
he left his walking stick. Maybe stop and roll a smoke, a little
rest would help. No pocket or blue denim shirt; instead, the
naked chest and hide thong holding a pouch. No Levi's and
boots, but barefoot with deerskin-wrapped loins. No lights
across the river where the houses nestle, no clearing of hay
fields and gardens. This must be a different place, he thinks,
and steps over a fallen branch which is a spider's web, a cable
thick and glistening. He walks the rounded cable, toe-clutch-
ing steady, head back to view stars, then eyes closed to sense
feet. Across the river and high over the treetops he's walking,

slowly walking, his voice a humming from a deep chest place, a song to stars and seasons. Song of spider, the weaving patterns of light behind eyelids, eyes turned inward to the voice in the cave of his mind.

A strange dancer lit by moon, the slowly revolving ladder to earth sways and curves with every movement. Rope ladder from the sky, the spider night is a dark belly. And then the odor of burning juniper and sage, and down slowly through the smokehole, down. His feet on hard-packed dirt and backward slowly to the waiting warm robe. Upon his back now he watches the ladder slowly being pulled back to sky, and the sky is a smokehole circle. His body is numb, and only his eyes can move to take in the circle of the roundhouse with sparks and smoke, another enclosed sky world.

It is a dream, then, nothing more. A memory, not a voice, has suggested that he keep his special anger in a dark corner of this round room. It might be tiny chirpings his mind creates, but no, it is fire talking. Now Coyote is sitting by the fire, studying the sky worlds of each spark and lick of flame. A gourd cup filled with cool water, round, round gourd, rounded water reflecting smokehole and sky. A droplet of water on his wrist mirrors all else to eyes. He notices now the buckskin pouch hanging before him. It sways from shadow to light and back to shadow. Whatever is within is reaching his mind. His arms lift, and his hands cup, and his fingers gently touch the pouch. There is a warmth like a soothing, a power.

"Hey, Coyote!"

"Yes, that's what they say." He doesn't want to re-emerge.

The sunlight stabs a pain through eyes to brain. The windshield is misted with frost, and stone beads click together hanging from the rearview mirror. Someone is rocking the car and laughing. The taste in his mouth starts a stomach bile cough, and he opens the door to quickly suck in great gulps of air, clean air.

❖

Coyote running, running Coyote, sniffing the cyanide death trap of the game keeper's cunning; forever it seems, running, the snap and pop and frozen, teeth grinning death. Coyote hide thrown over barbed wire fence, the vulture on post is judge and jury; stiff and dirty hide, how do you plead? Where's the evidence, the witnesses, and what's the charge? Hmmm, yes, I see: devoured an Angus bull, four heifers, a broke-to-saddle mustang, and a 1930 Ford pickup. How do you plead? Hell, how'd I get this bullshit job? I'm a vulture, I didn't kill him, I only ate his eyes and picked his bones.

Coyote trotting, vague shadow, trotting Coyote, nudging our gentle sleep; forever it seems touching the fringes of dreaming. Coyote stealing first fire, a moon bark between sage and sand, obsidian claws clicking the count of unrecorded graves. Coyote, his shadow upon muted lives, medicine song bark and herbs he spreads to all directions. Coyote, your burden basket of upturned sky as you trot upon star paws.

Coyote walking, walking Coyote, the city's streets are strewn with tattered lives, hollowed heart echoes resound painfully emptied. Coyote walking, sniffing in occasional boredom, here a lamppost, there a hydrant, someone's leg, a quick jet of piss. Ignoring city dogs too peopled in their lust. Stopping to read scraps of paper, candy wrappers, banana skins, sticks, foil, cigarette butts; finding more truth in this miscellaneous mosaic than in any sacred tabloids cut to accommodate a shriveled mind.

Coyote resting close-eyed and backside to a university wall. Scholastic dreams hold little interference, a scrap of paper with embossed seal to fashion into tiny boats and set afloat. Legs twitch in sleep that would the mountains trot again.

❖

Elderberry Flute Song

He was sitting there on a stone
    at world's end,
all was calm and Creation was
    very beautiful.
There was a harmony and a wholeness
    in dreaming,
and peace was a warming breeze
    given by the sun.

The sea rose and fell
in the rhythm of his mind,
and stars were points of thought
    which led to reason.
The universe turned in the vastness
of space like a dream,
a dream given once and carried
    forever as a memory.

He raised the flute to lips
sweetened by springtime
and slowly played a note
which hung for many seasons
above Creation.
And Creation was content
in the knowledge of music.

The singular note drifted
    far and away
in the mind of Creation,
to become a tiny roundness.
And this roundness stirred
to open newborn eyes
and gazed with wonder
at its own birth.

Then note followed note
in a melody which wove
the fabric of first life.
The sun gave warmth
to waiting seedlings,
and thus were born
the vast multitudes
from the song
    of a flute.

PETER BLUE CLOUD (Aroniawenrate), is a
Native American, Turtle Clan, Mohawk Nation
at Caughnawaga. Former ironworker.

Edited: Alcatraz Newsletter in 1969. Poetry
editor for Akwesasne Notes 1975-76.

Now living with family in California, odd-
jobbing, wood-carving and writing poetry and
stories.

Books include: *Alcatraz Is Not An Island*
(Editor), Wingbow Press, 1972; *Coyote and
Friends,* Blackberry Press, 1976; *Turtle, Bear
and Wolf,* Akwesasne Notes Press, 1976; *Back
Then Tomorrow,* Blackberry Press, 1978;
White Corn Sister, Strawberry Press, 1979.

BILL CROSBY, the illustrator, was born and
raised in Lincoln, Nebraska and received his
B.F.A. from the University of Nebraska. He
presently lives and works as a carpenter in the
Sierra foothills of California with his wife,
Cindy and daughter, Jennifer.